VANILLA

BILLY MERRELL

VANILLA

SCHOLASTIC INC.

Copyright © 2017 by Billy Merrell

This book was originally published in hardcover by PUSH in 2017.

All rights reserved. Published by PUSH, an imprint of Scholastic Inc., *Publishers since 1920.* SCHOLASTIC, PUSH, and associated logos are trademarks and/or registered trademarks of Scholastic Inc.

The publisher does not have any control over and does not assume any responsibility for author or third-party websites or their content.

No part of this publication may be reproduced, stored in a retrieval system, or transmitted in any form or by any means, electronic, mechanical, photocopying, recording, or otherwise, without written permission of the publisher. For information regarding permission, write to Scholastic Inc., Attention: Permissions Department, 557 Broadway, New York, NY 10012.

This book is a work of fiction. Names, characters, places, and incidents are either the product of the author's imagination or are used fictitiously, and any resemblance to actual persons, living or dead, business establishments, events, or locales is entirely coincidental.

ISBN 978-1-338-10101-0

10 9 8 7 6 5 4 3 2 1   19 20 21 22 23

Printed in the U.S.A.   23
This edition first printing 2019

Book design by Nina Goffi

For anyone who's ever felt vanilla.
And for Nico.

WHAT IT'S LIKE WITH HUNTER

He calls me Vanilla
and presses his warm nose to my neck.
I don't know what to do but laugh
and let him.

He sniffs and smiles and tells me
I smell like myself.
Says it like an inside joke
until it becomes one.

I feel him there, his touch
settling against my skin.
His gentle arms
circling my shoulders.

It's as if a part of me has come loose,
but instead of spinning off into space
it turns back and stares at me
so sweetly.

"Vanilla," he says, and I press my smile to his.

He could say anything after,
and it would seem a compliment.

Like a backward sigh,
he draws me in. Holds his breath.

EARLY DAYS

As easy as it feels being Vanilla's boyfriend,
it was hard being friends at first.
He'd come over to hang out
and his eyes would scan my room,
making their way around
like a sweeping clock hand.
And I couldn't help but tense up,
wondering if he was smart enough
to figure me out.

When our eyes met again,
he'd change the subject.
It was always video games
he wanted to play, anything
as long as he didn't have to
look at me. And if I looked at him,
he'd ask me, "What?"
as if I wasn't allowed to look
without a reason.

One afternoon, after a big test,
when he'd been too busy
to see me all week,
I invited him over
with something in mind.
I said, "I'm tired of games."

We were almost teenagers,
and as many other friends as I had,
I'd chosen Vanilla to *really* know.
"Let's talk," I said,
but it turned into silence.
"Let's dance, then," I said,
putting on music.

"You mean, together?" he asked.
"Yeah," I said. "Get up."

He looked at me like I was crazy.
So I danced alone, holding back at first,
then not caring.
Vanilla tilted back and forth, still sitting,
an embarrassed metronome.
His eyes were locked
on my dresser mirror.

"I don't know what I'm doing," he said.
I pulled him up onto his feet, said,
"Then it's a good thing you have me!"
My left hand took his right,
my right took his left.
It occurred to me then
that I was definitely gay.
And following that thought was the thought
that I might be in love with my maybe best friend.

Vanilla sighed, then stood taller,
becoming comfortable
with my hands in his.
"You make it look so easy," he said,
watching my feet.
"It is easy," I said. "It's the easiest
once you let go and ride the music."

He turned to face the mirror,
letting go of my hands.
I told him not to be self-conscious.
"I'm intimidated," he said,
and I took his honesty as a good sign.
"Don't be," I told him. "I dance in here all the time."
"Practice makes perfect," he said,
calling me perfect.

His back to me, I looked in the mirror to see him
closing his eyes, committing to the dance.
The diva was breaking it down, losing herself
as if she didn't care about hitting the notes at all.
But Vanilla was still wiggling, tense,
trying to make a wave
instead of riding one.

"I think it helps to pair some part of your body
with some part of the song," I offered.
I put my hands on his shoulders,
pulsing the blips and bleeps into his bloodstream.
Vanilla stomped his feet to the swelling beat.

"Yeah!" I encouraged, and he clapped.
It was a bit off,
but at least he was smiling.
The song had a snare drum,
and Vanilla rocked
back and forth to its hiss,
opening his eyes,

catching my appraisal
in the reflection.

"You're not dancing?" he said,
and I realized I'd stopped.

Without missing a beat, I threw my hands up,
and matched my steps to his.
I threw my head side to side as the vocals intensified,
not knowing if he was watching,
but hoping he was.

As the song wrapped up, Vanilla asked for another.
So I skipped to an old favorite.
I mouthed the opening lines, pointing straight at him,
willing him to be comfortable.
I figured if I made myself the bigger fool,

Vanilla might follow me all the way
into oblivion.

"Nice," he said, copying my moves.
The song was winding down,
and I suddenly wished I'd played something longer.
"See?" I said. "You're a natural."

"Thanks to you," he told me,
dancing a little closer,
boyfriend distance, not friend distance.
I guess it startled me, because he apologized.
"No," I told him. "It's okay."
But we stayed apart as the song ended.

"Do you know other ways to dance?"
Vanilla was looking through the songs on the playlist.
"Like slow stuff?"
I watched his finger scroll.
"Pick a song and I'll happily dance to it," I said.

When he did, it was a crooner.
I swayed like a sea, like underwater leaves,
and Vanilla swam around me like a fish, making fun.
When we were face-to-face,
he took my hands again,
my right in his left,
his left in my right.
"Like this," he said. "Teach me."

I put my hand on his waist, like I'd been taught,
and moved his up to my shoulder. He looked down,
his eyes tracing my arm to his waist.
Then we both stared at our socks
as we felt, together, for the beat.

OUR SECRET LANGUAGE

"You're burning up," I said,
the first time we danced,

because he was blushing so hard
that I knew

what we were doing
was worth being done.

I could barely name it,
but it felt good,

nagging deep inside
like a kinship.

I didn't want to tell him
I saw him blushing,

because if he stopped dancing,
a part of me would stop

right on with it.
So,

"You're burning up," I said.
And to this day, if we're at a dance

or walking
or even standing still

and I want him suddenly
to spin me,

I only need to say those words.

THE SLEEPOVER

1

It stung like a hammer on nail,
but also built us. He said, "No." Said, "Never."
And I wanted to change him.
Already I knew I could.

We slipped into my sleeping bag
and kissed like the meeting of two wings
trembling out of their cocoon.
The room no longer fit.

I watched the two of us giggling,
holding tight, like it wasn't me there,
like I didn't deserve it.
We were taking off.

2

I was so in love with him already
that I took his word, *never*,
and held it against my heart
like a hand over a candle.

And for the first time, it didn't add up.
I wanted so badly to be looked at like that
by a boy. By him.
To be cherished—that's the word—

and loved and kissed.
Both of us
a part of
the same feeling.

I looked in his eyes but this time
he didn't look back. I could tell.
"I love you," he said, but he wanted it returned.
"I love you, too," I said,

wanting to be his echo,
to feel his words in my throat.

3

"But," I said,
"never come out, not ever?"
He looked so afraid. And I knew
I could be bravery for us both.

"Here," I said, and I found some paper.
He rolled against the wall, playing dead.
"Pros and cons. Go," I said.
But Vanilla just sat there.

"Pro, I could love you like this
in front of people," I said.
"Con," he said,
"people will make fun of us."

"No they won't," I told him.
"Not the people
we care about."
But I wrote it down anyway.

"Pro," I said,
"we wouldn't have to use our silly code for everything."
But, "Con!" he said. "I like our code."

He wanted to kiss,
but I was serious.
I needed him
to hear me.

"Stop it," I said. "Listen."
He crossed his slender arms,
and I caught a whiff
of his sweet smell.

The buzz ran through me
like electricity made of blood.
"Pro, if people knew,
I could do all sorts of things.

I could put up a shrine to you, a freaking altar.
And everyone could stop asking what I'm so happy about,
'cause they'd all know. Officially. Plus, let's face it.
They all suspect."

"You're not writing all of that down, are you?"
Vanilla was hugging his knees to his chest.
"Boyfriend altar," I said, writing it slow,
doubling every pen stroke for effect.

4

We were both quiet for a long time.
"Your turn," I said. And what I meant was,
it was his turn to make his case,
to put me in my place, maybe.

"Pro," he said,
"it will make you happy."
"I want it to make *you* happy," I told him,
and he said, "Exactly!

Everything you do
is like that. As if my happiness
is all that matters. But
what about yours?"

And my first thought was to correct him.
Aren't they the same? I thought,
feeling again
like wings.

He let go of his knees finally,
unclenched his body, kind of.
I sat upright, following his lead.
"Really?" I said. "Can we? Please?!"

"I mean, not right this second," he said.
"I want your mom to let me sleep over."

And as we laughed, I swear
a glow-in-the-dark star
fell straight down onto us
off my ceiling.

It felt like another sign,
even to Vanilla,
who claims he doesn't believe in signs,
even after all we've been given.

5

"Before the dance," he said. "I promise."

6

The next day I found that star
right there in the sleeping bag.
I put it on my dresser
and folded our list into a paper heart.

I took the candle from the hall bathroom,
lit it, and sat there, all quiet,
with my hands barely touching.
I was only a little bit scared,

and feeling less and less so by the second.
Because now I had a purpose
other than to love him well.
Frightening as it was, I'd gotten my way.

MY FAVORITE PART (OF THE DAY)

is when we get to Hunter's apartment after school,
and his mom's not there, and his phone's almost dead.
He plugs it in and we take off our shoes,
having said everything there is to say
already on the walk.

Hunter turns the TV on. I unravel
one controller, then another,
and plug them into his dad's old game system,
while Hunter moves the back cushions from the dirty sofa,
making room for us both to lie parallel.

We'll start off upright, playing a round or two,
fighting each other or teaming up against a boss.
I can tell Hunter's mood based on the game he picks,
and for a while it feels like real life, real fighting.
Then it doesn't, and I can relax.

That's not the part I like.
My favorite part comes after,
when I get tired and quit,
and lie with my head in his lap.
I can hear his pulse,
my ear hot against his thigh.

If he tires first, he'll put his legs across mine.
Which always hurts, bony as his knees are.
I'll lift his legs and let them crash down with a bounce.
Then I'll lie down beside him, nuzzling deep,
Hunter's chest to my back as I lose the game.

But so what?
His arms come around me,
and I feel entirely at ease.

His nose parting my hair
as he falls asleep.

It's like I'm alone,
the only one in the world awake.
And I love it.
Him both there and not. Feeling
the pulse of his breath

and making it *our* breath
by matching mine to his.
The way his warmth becomes mine,
his shape mine as we lie like a landscape,
body and breath, land and sky.

Close,
yet blissfully separate.

TICKLISH

Running in the rain one day, I take in the perfection
as each splashing step hits asphalt.
I smell the perfume of the wet dead grass
as he takes my hand, licking rivulets from his top lip.
We dash through the parking lot, cutting a diagonal
to my building's door. And then we breathe, laughing,
lightning striking far off, as the rain falls harder.

Our shirts are soaked through and clinging.
My jeans are sopping wet, so tight
I struggle to pry my key from my pocket.
My clothes feel heavy. My socks are stained
with bleeding colors from my cheap-ass shoes.
He waits in the doorway as I drip off to the bathroom
to get towels. By the time I return, my pants are gone,
my shirt is gone, I'm wearing nothing but wet boxers.
He's shivering, chattering his teeth.

I dry his hair, my own still dripping.
I peel his T-shirt over his head and hug him hard,
my towel between us. I rub his sides
and back until he's warm again. "Shhh."
The rainwater tickles as it navigates my back,
zigzagging against the tiniest hairs,
pooling at the elastic.
I imagine it's him, tickling me like that,
imagine it's his daring and not my own,
all but naked in front of him.

I watch as he struggles with his shoes and socks,
wrings them out in the sink.
I tell him I'll put his pants in the dryer.
"That's okay," he says. "They're almost dry."
He runs the wet towel up and down his legs.

He can't stop staring at my boxers,
at the tent of the wet fly.

"Whatever you say," I huff, not buying it.
He inches his jeans off, and his briefs down after them,
covering himself so I can't see. One leg at a time,
struggling to keep the towel up
until he's naked underneath.
I pull my boxers off,
not bothering to hide. I smile
as he looks. As he blushes. "I'll get you
another towel," I tell him, putting our clothes
in the dryer. They pound and clang,
rivets hitting the barrel walls.

"This isn't so bad," I whisper,
swaddling him, my knuckles
grazing his naked chest.
"Yeah," he says, swallowing.
I can hear our hearts pounding
in time with the laundry,
can feel him getting hard between us.
"What?" I say, wanting him
to say it. To say anything.
But his eyes are closed
as he shakes his head,
blushing. "No. What?"
I'm flush, too. But not
from embarrassment.
I'm naked in front of him,
but pressed so close
he can't see. Only feel.

I knew this might happen.
When I least expected it,
when I stopped waiting.
I put my lips to his and his mouth
opens. He lets my tongue

wet his own. Grips my damp hair
at the back of my head.
I glide a warm hand
all the way down his back.
I stroke his sides, his ribs
and nipples. He lets me
kiss his neck, behind
his ear. "I love you,"
I say, my lips
buzzing in his ear.
"Me too," he says
practically panting.
I reach to undo the knot
of his towel, let my thumb
graze his belly button.
And that's when
it happens: He pulls
away, giggling, "Stop,"
claiming that it tickles.

THE INVITATION

They're known throughout the school as The Gang.
They aren't violent. They don't hurt anyone or
break anything—other than hearts.
But they're bullies, plain and simple,
even if not the obvious kind.

They bully us with their bodies,
always shirtless, always loud.
Roving, in heat. Gay as it gets.
And everyone has to know it.

At school, they flirt with anyone, even the jocks.
Because they're jocks, too—could be, anyway—
so they can stand up to anyone. And do.

After school, they go online together
and parade themselves.
Though not everyone sees, everyone talks about it.
In that way, too, I'll call them bullies,
always insisting on being talked about.

Once I got a group text, inviting me to an "exclusive" party.
But every gay guy at school got it, out or not.
And there The Gang was, on the invite,
all lined up in their birthday suits.
I didn't look. Okay, I did.
But I didn't go to the party.

I try to imagine lighting a wildfire on purpose.
Because that's what they do.
Sometimes I see one of them in the hall
and he looks at me, like, *I know you've seen my dick.*
And that's how they bully us, too.

Hunter and I have agreed
in no uncertain terms
that we'll never be like them.

Then one day,
after school,
we see them hitchhiking, or pretending to.
Sticking out their thumbs, steps from campus,
as if they'd get into the first car that stopped.

When they see us, they wave. One comes over—
we all call him Abercrombie, because of his muscles.
"What are you boys up to?" he asks.

"I don't know, the usual," Hunter says,
sounding cool.

He's always nicer than I am.
He laughs at their weird jokes
and pretends to swoon at their flirting.

But every time I'm around them, I think,
When can I get out of here?
Someone will see us talking to The Gang.
And then I won't be able to say, "Ew,
I don't talk to those guys."

"Hey, Huntress," Clown says, overhearing us from afar.
He takes out a compact, checks his face.
Clown is their ringleader, their founder.
He's the one who posts,
tagging us all in the photos,
even though we aren't in them.
"What's 'the usual' for you ladies? Shopping?"

"No," Hunter says. "Video games, probably."
He turns to me for confirmation.
But before I can do so much as nod,
Clown comes at us,

nodding fast, lips pursing
as his eyes scan my boyfriend
right in front of me.

"What's it to you?" I say.

"She speaks!" Clown shrieks,
as if he'd been fishing for it.
They all come over.
"She speaks!" The Gang chants,
forming a circle around us.

"What was that, Vanilla? You have words?"
Abercrombie taunts.
But I don't. I just want to go.

"Compliment their shoes," Hunter whispers
loud enough for them all to hear.
They laugh, all but Clown,
who's shooting daggers at me
with his big brown eyes.

He wags his finger in Hunter's face.
"Pussy Riot over here has words on Privacy.
I want 'um!" Clown snatches at the air between us.
"I know you have a problem with me. Say it. *Speak.*"

"I don't have a problem with you," I say,
not wanting any trouble.
"She speaks!" Abercrombie starts chanting again,
but Clown wants Silence!

"Speak, Vanilla. Give me your treatise on Privacy, gurl."

"I'm not a girl," I say,
figuring I'll be safe
as long as I stick to facts.

"We're all a little bit girl, gurl."
Clown stomps his heel,
whips his head around
as if he has long hair.

"You are, maybe," I say.
"Doesn't mean I am."

"Oh, I am.
Definitely,
gurl."

The Gang flashes one another their sign,
pretending to jerk off two fingers.

"Okay, bye," I say, ready to go.
Hunter looks at me like I'm being rude, says,
"Give him a break, ladies. He's new."

"Bitch, please," Clown squeals.
"You two have been married
since the seventh grade.
Show me that ring again?"

Clown reaches for my hand,
but I pull away.

I look at Hunter, want him to save me.
But Clown has already lost interest.
He flits his long eyelashes at Hunter.

"What's it gonna take
to get you to come?" Clown says,
and The Gang laughs.

"Come where?" Hunter says, soaking up their attention.

"Halloweeeeeen," Clown says. "Ab's house."
The Gang goes on cooing, hollering at cars,

unbuttoning and re-buttoning
each other's shirts. But Clown stands there,
locked on Hunter as if he's capable of mind control.
"I dare you," he says.

"Yeah," Hunter replies. "Maybe."
Then he reaches for my hand
as if holding it makes everything okay.
But instead it makes it worse.
I mean, it might as well be Clown reaching for me.

That's how hard
I pull away.

WHAT IT'S LIKE WITH VANILLA

Sometimes he holds my hand back.
Sometimes he hugs me for longer than a second.
Sometimes, late at night,
when I'm feeling lonely and stupid
for no reason and am too old to be held
but need so badly to be, right then,
he answers and listens
and agrees to pretend
that I'm lying there with him.
And sometimes, lying there,
pretending, I tell my dream boyfriend, "No,
you're perfect, maybe,
but you're not real,
you're not mine."

I think of Vanilla and how vanilla he is,
and I want to hold him and tell him
it's okay if he says he isn't ready,
even if I don't believe him—
or that if he isn't ready,
it's for all the wrong reasons.

Vanilla doesn't want to have sex
because after sex
comes more sex, along with conversations
about what we want
and who we are, and how we know
what's enough, and
*Please, love me forever despite
everything*
And *Love me, forever, now
that I have nothing new to give
and never will.*

At least, that's what he thinks
he'll think, after.
As if either of us knows
how deep that well is,
never having thrown
a penny in for ourselves.
Having only listened
to the splash and laughter
of other people's wishes.
Not knowing if they came true or not,
'cause no one says, later.

We've been together for so long
it no longer feels like a race.
Yet it hurts when others pass us.
It makes my chest tight
when I defend him, as if it's his voice
passing through my throat.

Maybe that's what love is, though:
taking on a little of another person's perspective
and holding true to it.

But there are days I can't deny
it feels like him I'm fighting.
He leans in for a kiss and I pull him into me,
holding his body against mine
until I can feel his blood quicken.
When he tries to pull away, I hesitate.
As if to overpower him
might feel like winning.

There are days I breathe him in so deeply
I can taste him when I swallow,
afraid of never getting a real taste.

And I confess,
those days when he pulls away

that rejection
feels as much like always
as our love does.

LUST AT SEVENTEEN

It's hard enough—pardon the pun—
that the world is constantly reminding me
I have a penis.

Everything in the adult world is sex.
And everything in my world
is also. Is more so,

except it's officially less so.
Being that I'm not an adult by law,
only by raging instinct.

If that makes sense.
That doesn't make sense,
thinks my brain.

Nothing makes sense,
thinks my dick,
thinking only of what it can touch

with its skin—
if you can even call it that.
It doesn't feel like skin, not always.

Nothing like the skin everywhere else,
feeling outward, proud of its purpose,
knowing the world

for what shapes and textures present themselves.
The skin of my penis knows almost nothing.
All it knows is me,

which isn't much—
and feels like less and less
the more my penis realizes

who else might touch it,
if they only would.

I touch the skin on my wrists together.
It isn't the same. It just isn't.

It's not like the skin on my elbow. Or behind my knee.
Nor is it like the skin of my lips, inside or out.
My mouth tastes. My tongue savors.

And my penis does nothing.
Maybe rubs fabric,
staying put.

High five, penis!
Way to wait it out!
Oh, wait. People are looking.

But later, sir. You'll get what's coming—
pardon the homonym.
And so will I.

HOPELESS ROMANTIC

Seriously, though.

I will.

Right?

WHY IS EVERYTHING ABOUT SEX?

My aunt says she doesn't have a problem with gay people,
only with what they do.

When I ask what she means, explaining that we're not
all the same, she says, "Yes, you are."

She laughs when she says it. "You know what I mean."
But I honestly don't.

And maybe that's why
I don't want to. Afraid

of making her right
when she's always so wrong.

"Why are you so scared of sex?" I ask her,
and it's like I'm asking myself.

Innocent. Not even daring.
But she slaps me anyway.

Not hard. It barely hurts. But my mother
stands up at the table, and everyone apologizes.

Everyone but me.

"Being gay isn't only about the sex part," I explain.
I don't understand why the statement confuses them.

Even Hunter, on the phone, after my family is sleeping.
"Not all gay people have sex, but it's the sex part

that makes us gay," he says, as if I'm not gay
until I have sex with him. As if we aren't a couple

without coupling.
"You do want it eventually,

even if you're not ready yet," he goes on,
but I'm tired of talking about it.

I fall backward onto my bed.
Stare blankly at the ceiling fan.

It's loose, so it shakes a little. Not enough to fall,
but enough that the little metal stopper on the cord

won't stop tapping the glass fixture,
like a steady, muffled bell.

"You do want it, though," Hunter says.

At first, as a statement.
Then as a question.

OUTSIDE PERSPECTIVE

When Hunter and I fight, we're quiet about it.
One of us nips, then the other.
It never lasts long enough to need waiting out.

With Red, though, there's a war history.
She won't stop until there are hurt feelings
and one of us has said something we can't take back.

But after every fight comes a feeling of lightness,
as if we're stronger for it,
having acknowledged something necessary, a thorn
that might be filed down.

"You only want to hang out if I'm paying," she'll say.
Or, "You never notice my socks."
And I'll know how to be better to her,
because she's told me how.

"You only talk about Hunter," Red says.
And I confess sometimes it's a struggle
to think of myself
and what's happening
and not think of him
as happening most.

"He can't be your boyfriend *and* your best friend," she says,
as if Hunter's the one being greedy, not me.
"*I'm* your best friend. Got it?" she says, and I nod,
unsure how to defend his standing without upsetting her.

"Just promise me you won't pick him over me
without *thinking* first, without considering
my side," she says. "I know I'm a bitch, but I'm worth it."

Hunter thinks Red simply likes the drama.
Red thinks there's a part of Hunter
that's afraid of being real in real time.

He fosters an air of knowing himself,
but there are parts of him off-limits, hidden even from me,
truths he only hints at in poems.

Red laughs when I read her one
about a closed flower leaning toward a bee.
"So many bridled horses," she says. "Towers. Doors!"

She says they aren't only metaphors
if he uses them over and over,
instead they're windows
into his soul.

Everything Hunter volunteers about his dad, his home life,
is curated, I realize. Typed out, cleaned up. Deemed
ready to be read. If the poems have windows,
they only show what he wants me to see.

"Whether you're the flower or the bee," she says,
"he's trying to get in your pants."
She thinks it'll bug me. But instead, it actually hurts.

WHAT IS HE SO AFRAID OF?

Look at me.

I'm like one of those birds that builds a nest
out of only blue things.
Blue glass, blue string,
all organized by shape.
Bottle caps. Shiny cracked beads.
Feathers and pebbles and lace.

Vanilla is always begging me to put stuff down
when I find it on the sidewalk
or along my trail in the park.

But I see something and it reminds me of him. Of us.
And I hold it for a while, afraid to put it down.

He looks both ways, even when there are no cars.
He walks so fast, crossing,
like he's afraid of walking on asphalt.

Once, when it was late
and the streetlights had only just come on,
I actually pulled him into the empty road
and made him stand there
with his arms crossed
as I hugged him.

I said, "Everything's okay.
Nothing's coming."

But it was like he didn't believe me.

"Can we get out of the road, please?" he begged.
I let go and walked him to his bike.

Love me, I thought as he rode off,
and I'll make a goal
of making every day of your life
a little better than the last.

I knew some of my charm might be homespun,
disposable, having served its purpose
after a single smile.
But some of it might be locked away forever
inside each other.

Then I heard his voice
calling from behind me.
"I feel it," he said. "The adrenaline."
I turned
and he was standing up on the pedals,
coming at me fast.
He shivered his shoulders,
skidded to a stop
next to me.

"What a rush," he said,
and I shook my head.
"It wasn't scary," I told him.

But in truth it was a little,
because of him.
I mean, what if he failed the test
and refused to trust me?
Or what if a car came,
startling us both?
I knew either way
there was a chance
one of us would ruin it.

And yet, if I read him right
how could I go wrong?

I have Vanilla all figured out.
He likes to be coddled and challenged at once.
He blushes and dodges but his eyes tell the truth.
They say, *Show me how to feel.*
As if he's afraid of himself for some reason.
As if it's never been in his nature
to dig into discomfort
for the change between its cushions.

Vanilla leaned off his bike to kiss my cheek,
like a prince bending down from his horse.

"You know," he said, "my parents always told me
that they knew they were in love with each other
when they couldn't imagine being with anyone else.
And that's how I feel, even though you scare the hell out of me."

"I'm not scary!" I said, making a joke of it.
I put my arms in the air, as if I was fed up.
Vanilla pulled them back down to my sides
and kissed me hard, not bothering to look around,
as if he didn't care who saw.

"Yeah, you are," he said, holding me tight,
tighter than either of us can hold ourselves.
But looking just as afraid
as he had in the road.
"I am, too, right?"

And I laughed and told him he was scary as it gets,
though I'd never felt safer.

"Tell me there's a part of you that was afraid," he begged.

HONESTY

How could I tell him   what I need
and not fear   his answer?

How could I tell him   his love
isn't enough   if fixed like a star   to follow?

I need to know we're going somewhere,
and weirdly   it doesn't quite matter   where

as long as I know   he's with me,
really with me   in heart and action both,

in want   and hope   and spirit.

"What does *ready* mean to you?" I ask him.

"To me   it means trust,"   I say,

"trusting we won't   regret it ever,
won't let the other down   or put the other in danger."

I tell him again that I'll love him   always
the way people seem only to aim for

and never to reach.   I tell him   he's the only reason
I believe in love at all.   But "I know" is all he says

because I've told him   probably fifty times   already.
"I need to know   you trust me," I say,

not wanting   trust to be   code for sex,

or mentioned ever again in this context.

It isn't sexy   asking for it.
Never having asked,   even I know that.
But thoughts can be a lot,   even ones pushed away.

I need him to know   he can't put me off   forever.
But also that it can't be me, again, urging him.

"I don't want to ask," I say. "It's always, always, me

who does the asking.   Please,

this time I need you to take the lead. It's the only way
I'll trust myself."   I look Vanilla in the eyes,

scary as it is,   and can tell he's heard me.

"You trust me that much?" he asks.
And I tell him that I do.

HIDING TOGETHER

To remember our first meeting
is to remember first feeling
surrounded.

A wall of honeysuckle.
White-and-yellow flowers
speckling a swell of green vines.

Imagine being alone
and hiding in that cloud all recess,
pulling stamens out like swords,
savoring the little sugar.
Then some other boy finds you there.

He's red-faced and out of breath,
and as startled to see you
as you are to see him.
He needs to hide, quick,
and can he hide with you?

Stare at him as he listens
for his friend counting backward
to zero. Stare at his dirty hands
and how he pushes them through
his curly, sweaty bangs.

Point to the honeysuckle flowers.
Watch him not understand.

Then silently pinch one off for him, show him how,
thinking, *Welcome.*
See that light in his eyes
that holds you, briefly,

as he puts the flower
to his mouth.

Still looking back at you
as he runs off.

HISTORY OF HURT

1

I knew this would happen
eventually.
One of us—him specifically—
would change

and we'd both know why—
specifically me,
always knowing what I want
and what I don't.

Why, when I love him,
can't I tell him
who all I am,
that what I need is a nest

and one guy to hold
and isn't it enough
to earn it over time
like anything good?

2

Hunter says, "Vanilla,
I can wait," says it every time now,
sniffing my neck for lotion. But
he gets so into it
that pulling him back from the brink
takes every part of me
and every part of him, it seems,
so we never part
on purely sweet terms anymore.

He kisses my cheek goodbye now,
as if he's afraid of kissing my mouth.

3

We've been kissing since before we were boyfriends.
Simply because we were alone, and it felt good
to be close to someone.
In his room, or mine.
In parked cars, waiting for one parent or another.

When Hunter kissed me early on,
it was comfortable and easy.
It felt right. Like a perfect hug
or a hat that finally knows the shape of your head.

The first time we kissed in public,
I was nervous that someone might see.
But Hunter reminded me it didn't matter.
We were at the fair, surrounded by strangers.
Hungry to show the world
the kind of joy we were made of.

"Kiss me," he said, and I thought he was kidding.
"I have mustard on my lips," I told him.
But there were fireworks, and everyone was looking up.
The explosions thundered overhead, but to us
it might as well have been applause.
"Come on," he said, and I looked around.
No one cared, except us—who cared so much.
So I did.

And again at the top of the Ferris wheel.
We kissed because we could,
and because that fact required celebrating.
Then we kissed because we liked the intimacy.
And because, why not?

I wasn't sure at first. I was nervous.
Hunter likes to remind me of that fact.
When I see his begging smile, slightly sweeter than he is,
something stirs, from way back when.
Trust him, a voice inside me says
when I'm not sure if I can trust myself.

I can close my eyes and feel the rush again.
Sometimes it's enough to make me dizzy.
As if we never get down from those first heights.

4

People ask me all the time
when I first knew that I was gay,

as if I realized all at once
in a flash, instead of slowly, over time—

a series of gut feelings, involuntary responses
to conversations, words, assumptions.

People ask and I've always had an answer ready.
I'd tell them the short version of our story—
which would inevitably lead to the long version.
We're the only couple we know
who have been together since middle school.

I've been proud of our longevity
but recently it makes me feel more like an outsider,
as if being together this long and falling in love
before sexuality became a part of it
puts us in a separate category.

One we didn't choose,
and one we're alone in,

uncomfortably.

5

Turns out there's a right word for everything.
A precise word with a precise meaning.
And I love, usually, how Hunter forages for it,
his finger trailing the alphabet.

He'll describe our favorite days as they're happening,
comparing the wood grain of my grandmother's dresser drawers
to that of a picture frame in the hallway, outside my bedroom,
or the surface of the lake to an old burnished coin
he saw once on my windowsill.

He'll point to the firework sparks, naming their color
after my go-to coffee mug. And I'll see it, briefly,
before the bright blue embers fade to smoke.

It's something at the time, for sure,
but later it's everything.

I'll catch myself loading that mug into the dishwasher
and I'll think of him again, and us, and joy.
Fireworks on lake water. His hand in mine in shadow.
The comfort that sneaks up on us.
I'll clean my room and find that coin
and clutch it until it hurts, until I'm sorry.

"Look, a balloon," he'll say. And sure enough,
darting up from over the suburban rooftops
is a green balloon, wild in the breeze.
And I'll say, "Green," and he'll say, "Spring green,
like new leaves." And for no good reason,
I'll push back, winding him up.
"More like lime green," I'll say.
"Limes don't shine like that," he'll tell me.
And I'll dare him
to point to a leaf as green as that balloon
free-flying toward the sun.
"Spring leaves are different," he'll say.

6

When we first met, we didn't know each other.
He wasn't in any of my classes, but I'd see him outside
during a shared free period, running and tackling
other boys, while I sat and read,
or played cat's cradle with the girls.
I'd notice if he smiled or not,
never saying anything, never
inviting myself along.

Hunter says we would have gone on like that forever
if he hadn't picked this girl for his seventh-grade lab partner
simply because he saw her talking to me.
Knowing that one day when she was sitting with me again,
he could run up and put his hands over her eyes,
the whole time staring into mine
as she giggled and guessed.

Hunter says we wouldn't have ever talked
if he hadn't waved me over by the bikes,
to ask if I wanted to go riding around sometime.
And he's right. Even after that, I know
he had to pull every word out of me,
like a magician pulling scarves out of an empty fist.
He'd write notes, and I'd savor them,
afraid to pass one back. And he'd come in late to lunch
with a fistful of crumpled honeysuckle flowers,
calling it dessert, then dashing away to his friends.

I knew the feeling was good, because I looked forward to it.
But it wasn't easy, feeling it. Not knowing how to answer,
afraid he'd give up on me if I didn't.

7

Caught in the rain, caught
chasing him to shelter.
His empty apartment, lightning

doubling far off. Ominous
and not, like his flashed smile.

And when we got inside, lights out,
he stripped like it was nothing.
Took his pants off, asked
for mine. It wasn't how
I pictured it, not ever.

His hair wet, his body maybe.
But my clothes that tight
felt like fitted armor
he removed, plate by plate
as I steeled myself

until, shirtless, limitless,
he put his warmth
like a wick to mine,
passing me his heat,
his very comfort

and I thought, *Yes, like this*.
It was the rain, we'll say.
I had no choice but to
take it all off. Blaming the cold
for our pressed bodies.

But, *No*, I thought. *Stop thinking*.
Stop with the walls, the logic.
Let him take you where he's going.
Fragile in his wet hands,
nestled in the river's drawl.

Knuckles like warm stones,
twinned hearts in agreement.
I could follow him downriver
as far as the current went,
if only he'd pull me, quick

as water, to water's end.
But instead, he asked me
to put words to it, thoughts.
No, I thought. *Not this again.*
"What?" And I drowned.

I shook my head, closed
my eyes. He was kissing my mouth
with his mouth, my back
with his fingers. I breathed
and waited for want

like a thirst beyond my tongue.
He was telling me, hand to nipple,
what he loved. Was spelling
it out on my open body.
Telling me with words

what I needed him to say
through me, silent.
I reached around and felt
how cold his skin had become,
giving his warmth to me.

And then, as if he wanted it back,
he was pulling me into him,
his fist at the tuck of my towel.
Hard where I was no longer hard.
Sure where I was no longer sure.

8

The Monday after his ultimatum,
Hunter surprises me with a film he's made
full of quotes and pictures,
telling me the reasons he loves me.

But I can't help but see the video differently now.
As if he's giving me reasons

I should love him more
and with my body.

I thought the trick to love
was finding the right person.
And that, after finding them,
all they have to do is truly know you.

Once they see all the way in,
how could they not love you?
How could you not love them back
for loving you enough to know you so well?

I guess I still think that.
Only now, he thinks there's more to know.
More than I'm sharing.
More to me than I know myself.

9

"What do you think?" Hunter says
when his movie's over and I still haven't said
that I love him. There's a familiar, pleading look in his eyes.

I think of the first time I broke Hunter's heart
on accident. How I was afraid I'd ruined everything,
like I could now.

It was seventh grade, before we were calling it dating.
We were hiding in a tube slide. I forget why.
Hunter insisted on wriggling up next to me with his camera,
claiming the light inside the slide was a good yellow.
I like yellow as much as the next person—which is to say, not much.
But it's Hunter's favorite color and always has been,
so I smiled at the idea of him having my portrait like that
and held the smile as long as it took, even though I knew
I'd look like an emoji smiley face,
with my too-round cheeks and dark round eyes.

Hunter pretended we were stuck, shimmying up against me.
He made a joke of it, though it didn't seem like a joke.
He inched closer, pressing into me. Then he closed his eyes
as if it were possible to sleep still smiling.

It didn't take him long to give up the charade.
But when he did, he wasn't smiling anymore.
He looked as serious as ever.
In fact, I remember thinking that something was wrong
when he turned to me in the tube,
static crackling between our bodies
and the plastic walls,
and kissed me.

We had kissed a million times before
but that was the first kiss I didn't understand.
I kissed him back a long time,
every thought disappearing in yellow.
It was only after, that I asked him.

"You seemed to like it," he said. "Sorry."
"I *do* like it," I said. "Don't apologize."

He told me he wished we'd been kissing like that all along.
Then, out of nowhere, he called me his boyfriend.

"I'm not allowed," I said, instinctively,
because I wasn't. I wasn't allowed to date
until I was sixteen; my parents had *always* said so.

"I'm not allowed to date," I said, and he furrowed his brow.
"But we go on dates all the time," Hunter argued,
getting mad, like it was a bad joke.
"I don't call them dates," I said.
"I didn't know that's what they were."

"But I kissed you!" he said, like it was obvious.
Which might have been the case if he'd said it earlier.

Hunter was walking me to my bike. Carrying my backpack.
It all seemed so romantic suddenly

and yet it was all too much
for my parents to take.
For me to take, even.

"I can't," I said,
but I still wanted a kiss.

I leaned in, hopeful.

The look on Hunter's face, denying me then,
is the same face he's making now,
waiting for me to pay him back
for his dumb movie.

A KISS IS JUST A KISS

There's the problem of telling Vanilla what I want
and then there's the problem of having told him.

It's the having told him that haunts me worse,
now that every kiss we share seems like a trap to him,

as if I mean to lure him in,
using my tongue as a hook.

LONG GAME

His love is like a pine, fixing the ground
so nothing else will grow.
His love waits like a pine waits,
throwing bombs down
and helicopters.
Vanilla won't stop unless I climb—
except he has no limbs
low enough
to the ground.
And when I try,
he blames me for trying.
And when I don't try,
he blames me for giving up.

In his version of our meeting, Vanilla makes all sorts of claims.
That I was playing hide-and-seek while he was eating flowers.
That I hid with him and he got me drunk on nectar.
But it was freeze tag. And I wasn't hiding from anyone.
I just saw him there, alone by the honeysuckle,
perfectly content all on his own.
I thought, that could be a good friend.
This boy who doesn't want to be chased.
Doesn't throw first punches, begging for it.

In the park near my apartment, there's a patch of brambles
the two of us could sneak behind.
It's there I planted a stolen vine.
The very honeysuckle
at which we met.
For two years now
I've been training it.
And sometime next summer,
I'm going to take Vanilla to our new spot
and kiss him there, surrounded by honeysuckle flowers, ours.

I imagine more, too.
But the kiss will be enough, if it has to be.
Or the surprise on his face.
Or the taste of those flowers,
reminding us
who we were
and still are.

It's fine if his love is like a pine,
rocketing upward. I want his pulse
to drum the air between us
as we savor what little sweetness, et cetera—
but without him thinking I'm counting down, always.
Without his story being that I needed him
as much as he needed me. When in truth,
I just knew what I wanted.

His love is like a pine.
Fast and tall and quick.

His love is like pine,
pale and soft and so slight.

His love is like a pine,
useful wood, but is it rare?

I want love to be oak,
slow and steady, but sure.

I want our love to be that love.
Only less like his. And more like mine.

COUPLE'S COSTUME

1

"What do you want to be, my love?
Something cool or something bad?
Scary or sexy or both at once?

Do you want to make people laugh
at how wild our hair can look?
Or do you want to be a puzzle

no one quite gets, until they all do?
Life of the party or butt of the joke?

All I know is
it has to be great!" I say
as I lean in to kiss him.

"Why don't you worry about yours,
and I'll worry about mine,"
Hunter says, not even a question.

" 'Cause that's no fun. We're a couple!"
I say it tenderly,
worried something is wrong.

"Halloween's the one night
we can be anything we want," he says.
"Why would we pick
what we already are?"

Ouch.

"Whatever you want," I say,
wondering if he isn't just hungry.

"I want to go to Clown's party," he says.
I tell him, "Whatever you want, except for that,"
reminding him about Red's,
how I promised we'd go.

"She's my best friend," I say.
"You barely know those guys."

"*You* barely do," he says,
as if he's been friends with them all along
and I've failed to notice.

"I want them to like us," he says.
But why? He didn't care before.
So why now?

2

I lose the fight
by refusing to fight.
Go figure.

My first-ever
all-gay
party.

And the first real argument I've had with Red
in which I know from the beginning how wrong I am.
She hasn't texted back in two days,
and I wish I could say it's all I can think about.
But all I can think about is Clown's party,
and how embarrassed I'm going to be,
watching them strip and grind
and god-knows-what-else. Reminding Hunter
what he's waiting for.

Even as we park the car, even as we get out, step carefully
across Abercrombie's yard, strewn with poster-board gravestones
scrawled with teachers' names. Even after we're startled

by a motion-sensing zombie witch that pops out and screams.
Look who it is, Hunter says, but I'm oblivious.
They've dressed her in school colors, replaced her hat with a tiara.
But all I can think about are the photos I'll be in tomorrow,
blushing in the background. Looking so out of place.
Imagining the jokes Hunter will make, covering for me.

Hunter rings the doorbell, and I want to hide behind him.
But before the door has a chance to open, he turns to me,
looks me in the eyes, and thanks me.
"I'm sorry Red's mad," he says. "We'll make it up to her."
It's the *we* I cling to, ringing the bell again. We wait and listen.
A deep bass beat is drumming through the closed door.
When no one comes for us, Hunter checks his phone.

"We're here," he says into it, then hangs up.
A minute passes, and the same anonymous beat thumps on.
Hunter checks, and the door's unlocked, so we enter,
not knowing what awaits us in the noise.

There's a smoke machine and black lights.
Neon spiderwebs. Bowls of candy. But where is everyone?
They better not jump out at us, I think. Imagining Clown
in a fishnet something, coming at me with a pitchfork.
The rest of them taking video of my reaction.
But as we turn the corner, I see that everyone's out back,
drinking around a keg in the floodlit yard. Clown and his
extended posse. A chaos of voices, competing with the music.

There's a moment where it's Hunter and me inside,
watching them through the sliding door.
Then he's opening it and I'm wishing he wasn't.
The Gang is wearing matching kilts, nothing underneath.
They flash one another, already drunk.
When Clown sees Hunter, he squeals and puts his hands up high.
He's shaved his armpits. Rouged his knees.

"Hi," Hunter says, hugging them all
while I stand there.

A shark comes up to me. I don't recognize him.
He says, "What are you guys, *Jurassic Park*?"
They all look at me for the answer,
but at the exact same time that I say, "Yes,"
Hunter answers, "No, he's a fern.
And I'm a dinosaur."

"You two need to get your story straight," says the shark,
shaking Hunter's hand, then mine.
"Nothing's straight here," cries Clown, and all the boys toast to it.
Hunter mimes like he's handing me a cup,
and we join in on the toast, pretending to drink.

The shark has a deck of cards.
"Let's play FUBAR with the punch,"
he says to Clown, and Clown agrees.
A group of us go inside,
where it's too loud to talk or hear
more than a word or two.

Before I know it, there's a skull full of booze in my hand
and Hunter's drinking beer out of a huge glass boot.

"You good?" he asks me over the music,
holding the boot with both hands,
looking so proud to be there.
I nod, hoping I've heard him right.
But honestly I don't know how I am.
My every sense has been assaulted
by strobes and bass, vape smoke blown into my face.
There's a guy in a kitten mask sitting cross-legged in the living room.
He's been stripped down to his underwear—or is that his costume?
Twin drag queens spin around him in their metallic gowns,
mouthing the words to a song I've never heard.

"FUBAR!" The Gang screams.
Then Clown draws a queen.
"Drink, bitches," he says,
like he lives to raise his hand.

According to the rules,
"ladies" have to drink,
which at one of Clown's parties
means whoever he calls "she,"
or who in Clown's estimation
is "the girl of the couple."
Which, for the record, is NOT a thing.

Red would be furious, I think.
And then I block her from my mind.

Ab draws a jack, and The Gang does their sign,
taking shots of a thick white liqueur.
Clown sneaks one to Hunter,
his finger pressing to his lips
like it's a real secret.

I take smaller and smaller sips of punch,
afraid Hunter will need me to drive later.

"You call that chugging?" Clown says to me
when I don't feel ready for a full guzzle
after drawing an ace.
"Be fun," he says, his arm wrapping
around Hunter.

"This *is* me being fun," I say.

"It's true," Hunter says, sounding tipsy already,
and they all laugh, like it's funny.
"This is his upper range of fun right here actually."

It takes me way too long to realize he's making fun of me.
And the expression on my face must be hilarious
because no one in the room
seems able to breathe.

"Thanks," I say,
spreading anger onto everyone who's laughing.
But no one bothers looking at me.
They're all beaming at Hunter.

COUPLE'S COSTUME

3

We start by playing drinking games.
Everyone's having fun, even Vanilla.
But two boots in, I'm already tipsy.

"You look cute," Vanilla tells me, pulling me aside.
He tugs at the felt teeth attached to my hoodie.
But he's looking at Clown, not me.
He's performing for him.

"You look cute, too," I say. "Tropical."
I curl my hands like dinosaur claws
and tickle Vanilla until his fern fronds shake.
Proving he's not the only one
who can put on a show.

"FUBAR?" he asks me, his lips dyed red.
"Definitely," I tell him. I lean in,
thinking, *I won't stop kissing him*
until all that dye is gone.
But the moment I slide my tongue
between his lips and teeth,
he pulls away.

"I thought you weren't going to get drunk," he says.

4

I make jokes. It's who I am. It's why he loves me.
Or at least why he puts up with me, I think.
But when I make a joke at Vanilla's expense,
he gives me a look like I'm cut off.

I put my empty boot down on the floor.
It's Clown's idea, not mine, to spin it.
His hand crossing my lap.
He's kneeling at my feet in his kilt, and it's funny.
But I breathe in instead of laughing,
for Vanilla's sake. For mine.
Clown stands, asks if I like his perfume,
holding his glittered wrist to my nose.

"Mm-hmm," I say.
I look at Vanilla, worried
as he watches the boot spin.
I know when people play this,
there's usually someone they want to kiss.
Others they hope they won't have to.
But it occurs to me I might be happy
kissing someone new,
never having had the pleasure.

But when it lands on me, it's Vanilla who spun.
He looks so happy, I make a show of it,
kissing him like I would if no one was watching.
Clown's lips tremble in a silent snarl.
Vanilla must see it, too, because he's smiling
into my mouth. Putting his hands
into the pockets of my hoodie.
And The Gang is oohing and aaaaahing at us,
as if we're the cutest thing.

Before I know it, we're all dancing.
The keg must be empty, because no one's outside anymore.
Everyone is pressed together in the living room.
Abercrombie takes his shirt off,
and everyone takes turns
signing his chest and back with a marker.
Someone hands the marker to Vanilla,
but he passes it to me.

"Is this what you wanted?" Vanilla asks me.
"Yeah," I tell him, because it is.

There are gay people all around us,
laughing and belonging. And here I am
signing Ab's abs with hearts and stars,
with Vanilla right beside me,
the two of us part of The Gang.

"Good," he says, like he means it.
But how could he?

5

I don't think Vanilla's drinking.
Ab hands him a cup, and he smiles, thanks him.
But moments later, I see him put it down.
"I'm cut off, but you aren't," I say,
wanting him as tipsy as possible.
And he tells me he'll drive, and I kiss his cheek,
picking up the drink he set down.

The doorbell rings. I'm the only one who seems to hear it,
so I make my way to the door,
Vanilla follows close behind, and I want to scold him for it.
At the same time, I understand.
As few people as I know here, Vanilla knows fewer.
I take his hand as I open the door.

"Trick or treat?" several voices say,
and when I look, it's a cluster of freshmen,
each dressed like a different member of The Gang.
Baby Clown has glitter lipstick, purple cheeks.
Baby Ab, a six-pack drawn onto his belly.

"Welcome," I say, dying to see Clown's face.
Then I take my phone out, letting go of Vanilla.
I run ahead, in time to take a stealth video
as the freshmen make their entrance.

Vanilla sneaks up next to me
as Clown takes Baby Clown by the ear.
"You call those heels?" he says.
"Don't stroll up in wedges
strapped to your hooves,
thinking you're impersonating me.
At least get the walk right!"

Then Clown lets go, and two queens strut.
Clown with Baby Clown behind him,
wobbling a crooked line,
clear through the living room.

"Drunk, gurl?" Ab asks.
And Clown spins around,
pointing that painted pinkie at him.

"I'm fine. You mind your business!
Everyone heard me say already,
nothing's *straight* at this party."

6

Vanilla won't stop holding my hand.
Win.

He smiles when I kiss his neck,
beams when pull him close.
Win. Win.

I don't care who he's performing for,
Clown or me. It's a glimpse of what it might be like.
Able to touch my boyfriend again
without him flinching.

We're standing by the hallway, watching the party,
my arms around Vanilla's waist,
his silk leaves tickling my skin.

"Thriller" comes on, and The Gang rallies,
lining up in rows to dance like zombies.
They must have practiced the choreography
because they lurch and shudder in perfect unison.

"Okay," Vanilla says. "I'm having fun."
And I'm not sure why, but it makes me tear up.
I press my eyes to the back of his head,
relief coursing through me.
I smile, kissing his hair, telling him I love him.
"By the way," he whispers, "you're burning up."
So it's my job to take his hand
right where it is
and spin him out for all to see.
All his fronds
flinging free.
Win. Win. Win.

7

Just when I think the night can't get better,
Ab tells us there's a room we can go to,
Vanilla and me. I thank him with a wink.
But Vanilla gives us away, saying too much
about what we do and what we don't yet
until Abercrombie excuses himself,
telling me, "Sorry, bud."

"What was that?!" I ask Vanilla, mortified.

"If we were going to leave the party,
we would leave the party," Vanilla says,
as if it's the room I'm angry about
and not his oversharing.
"We should leave," he says. "I'll drive."

A minute ago, I would have said yes,
eager to kiss him in the car, go home,
lie in bed, thinking of all the things we could do.

But Clown saunters up, his mouth agape.
"Tell me it isn't true," he demands.
I blush and he turns to Vanilla.

"FREE him, gurl," he says,
then walks away.

MY TURN TO WALK AWAY

I've been putting up with Clown all night.
Laughing at his jokes. Returning each of his blown kisses.
The Gang won't stop flashing Hunter,
probably because he won't stop laughing
every time they do it. His face turning red.

It must be so satisfying, turning him on,
because none of them can help themselves.
"Just 'cause you don't have any,
doesn't mean the rest of us can't," Clown says
when he catches me fuming.

"Have any what?" I ask,
not bothering to hide my annoyance.
Not knowing how to.

"You name it," Clown challenges.

"Oooooh" and "Ouuuch,"
Clown's boys say,
like trained buffoons.

The shark asks, "What I miss?!"
as if Clown and I are on the floor,
holding each other by the hair.

"Vanilllllla," Clown purrs,
and The Gang laughs
like a big shared mouth.
No amount of rolling my eyes
seems to be helping.
Clown points at me
with his painted pinkie.
Beckons me with it.

"Vanilla's so vanilla," he says,
and the shark says, "Yeah?"

"It's the perfect name for him," he says,
winking at me like I'm in on it.
"Such a sweet thing. So innocent."

And I know by how Clown says it
that he's calling me a prude.

I don't argue, but I'm not laughing.
"Am I wrong?" Clown asks me,
sliding his hands down the front of his kilt.
"Does Vanilla think I'm sexy? Oh my!"

Someone turns off the music.

Hunter's drunk and smiling so big
it's like he can't tell I'm mad.
Watching Clown make a fool of me.

"Vanilla thinks I'm GORGEous, don't she?
Vanilla wants my kissssses, don't she?"

"Needs Ooooh." Clown squints.
"Needs Nnnnnng," Clown groans.
"Needs Aw Oh Eeeee!"

He bites his thick bottom lip
and runs his palm down his tongue
and then down his chest. Back to his crotch.

Hunter's laughing louder than anyone.

"It's okay, baby. We know.
We've all been there," Clown says.
And then,
"Lucky for Hunter, I like leftovers!"

He says it like a snake, hissing in Hunter's face.
His tongue tasting Hunter's breath.

I push past them, out the door.
I wait on the front porch for Hunter
so we can finally leave.

Three minutes. Five.

I text, *Are you coming or what?*
And a moment later, they're all laughing.
I can hear bits of jokes
muffled through the door.
And the music comes back on.

I have your car keys, I threaten.
And when he doesn't write back, I leave.

IT'S COMPLICATED

It's complicated.
How the shadow of the Earth
perfectly covers the moon.
Or how a cell splits
and splits, twinning perfectly.
Or how Red manages
to untangle her headphones
with only one hand,
barely looking down.

But this? It isn't complicated.

I'm tired of defending Vanilla
when we're at a party
and he brags about our lack of sex.
A fact he volunteers
as if he's afraid of strangers
assuming the opposite.

"Not every couple has sex," he corrects.
"Being gay isn't only about sex.
Why is everyone so obsessed
with orgasms? And *talking* about them?"

I close my eyes
because it's me they look at, eyebrows raised.
It's me they pull aside later,
to ask—less if it's true
than what's the deal with him.
"Your boyfriend's a homophobe," they say.
Or, "Who does he think he is?!"
Because no one wants to feel defensive
at a gay party, where they thought they'd be free
from that kind of judgment, finally.

"What happened to you?" I ask him
when I pour myself into the passenger seat,
having called him back to Ab's driveway.
"When did you get so mean?"

He cries, and at first it makes me feel bad.
But I'm upset, too, and drunk, so I cross my arms
and double down, not caring if my words are slurred.
"I'm sex-positive, for the record," I tell him.
"You might have put yourself in charge of my virginity,
but you don't get to decide my beliefs."

"What are you talking about?" Vanilla asks,
as if it's coming out of nowhere.
As if me being drunk makes me automatically wrong.

Vanilla wants me to quote him, but I can't.
Dares me to return to him
the exact wording of his wrongdoing.
But I'm tipsy and I can't.

"I was too pissed to journal it," I say,
wanting so badly to be home already
and over the whole conversation.
Now that I've made my point.

"I'm sex-positive, too," Vanilla says,
like he's chasing me. When all I wanted
was a boyfriend who wouldn't need to.
"You're sex-phobic," I say,
because it's what I believe.
What he's all but called himself,
claiming not to be ready.
Even though he masturbates.
Even though he knows how he feels.
Even though he loves me.

Vanilla shakes his head, driving,
and the bright trails of tears
go crooked on his face.

I want to wipe his cheek,
but he swats my hand away.
He's never seemed so sure of anything.
It's weird.

He's telling me what he thinks about sex, and
love, and intimacy. He's talking fast
like he could talk about it forever.

But I stop him. I don't want to hear it.
Not tonight.
Not when I might forget it later.

"It's not fear," he says.
"It's complicated."

NOVEMBER 1

Hunter thinks everyone's laughing at him.

He thinks because The Gang knows,
everyone knows. And even if he's right,
who cares?

"Why is this the *one* thing
you can't make a joke about?" I ask him.

"Because it's constant," he says.

I thought *we* were the constant.

"I need you to hear me," he says,
so I listen to his voice and watch his face
and already in his eyes there's an answer.

Tears welling. The sight of it
startles me.

"I know I said I could wait,
but lately I wonder, what's the point?"

I tell him I'm the point,
the prize for his patience.

It's fear talking.
"I'll try," I say. "I promise."

"You shouldn't have to *try*," he says,
shrugging like it hurts to acknowledge it.

"I do have to," I argue. "And I will."

NOVEMBER 2

"Tell me again why you skipped my party," Red says.
But I've told her a hundred times that I'm sorry,
that I hated Halloween, that I don't want to talk about it.
"There were seriously no girls there, like literally none?"

"Abercrombie means well," I tell her. "But, yeah,
he's kind of single-minded in that way."
"Is he even single?" she says. And I shrug.
"He has a lot of boyfriends," I explain. "A few were there."

Red compares Ab to a girl in her own clique,
calls the two of us "evolved" for not having "sex brain" 24-7.
"I don't know how they get anything done,
all the energy they put into getting laid."

"And yet, here we are talking about it," I say,
wondering if it doesn't take more energy, obsessing.
"What would Ab do if the dyke squad showed up to his party?"
"I don't know," I confess. "Quarantine you in his garage?"

"I'm glad you don't hate women," she says,
and I smile. But something about it, it's like she's asking.
"What does Hunter say about it?" Red wonders.
I don't want to tell her how much he loved the party,

that I can see why, even.
"So you're in The Gang now?" Red asks me,
and I shake my head. "Hunter maybe," I tell her.
She laughs, like it's all so ironic.

"I don't want to hear about it," she says.
"I'm tired of talking about Hunter."
I haven't even told her about our fight yet,
haven't asked her for a shred of advice. But I agree anyway.

"You're a smart guy," she says.
"I'm sure you'll think of something else to talk about."

NOVEMBER 2

Vanilla passes me a note,
and it says we have to talk.
All day I picture it
going one of two ways.

Either he's finally ready
or he's finitely not.

And then the day ends
and it's just us. I ask where
he wants to talk, hoping
we won't really be talking.

But he says he's not sure where,
or if it's even worth talking about.

I snap, and—
not thinking—
I call him a tease.

Which he isn't, and even if he were,
I'd never call him that.
Except I just did. And now he's
really going to punish me.

SOME WORDS REGARDING VANILLA

I don't like names. I want to shake them off.
Hunter's and mine. And be nobody, for once.

When Clown calls me Vanilla, he's calling me boring.
He's saying what I do is boring because of what I don't do.

And I mind much less that someone like Clown thinks it
than I mind the reminder that Hunter thinks it.

Hunter calls me Vanilla, and a part of my heart still swoons.
There's love in a word of shared meanings.

But Clown calls me Vanilla, and I want to scream something shocking,
tell him he doesn't know how kinky I can be,

that Hunter doesn't know, and neither do I.
And what does Clown care anyway,

other than to figure out how kinky Hunter is?
Which is always on his mind, I'm sure. The way he looks at him.

VANILLA

I don't call him Vanilla because he's vanilla.
He isn't boring, not completely.

I call him Vanilla because I always have.
And because I like his smell.

Besides, vanilla the flavor isn't boring, isn't blank.
If it were, they wouldn't sell it.
It's not that vanilla lacks flavor.

In fact, it's *all* flavor.
A flavor so pure
that if you add even a little

of anything else
what we call it
changes.

Vanilla,
like vanilla,
is pure.

And I'd take him any way
he'd let me,
including like this,

with all our clothes on,
lying parallel on the couch
like always.

All the choices in the world, and there Vanilla is,
vanilla-ing out, never feeling lonely
no matter how alone.

Except
there I am,
lonely, pressing into him.

Always knowing where the line is.

THE HAIRCUT

I don't know why I buzzed my head.
But I did.

I locked myself in the bathroom,
unsure if the guard was long enough,

or if I would look good without bangs
covering my pimply forehead.

But Hunter smiled when I opened the door
and ran his hand over the bristles,

all but half an inch of my hair gone.

"You look so hot," he said. "You could
be in The Gang." And I smiled,

relieved I was "hot" to Hunter
and not "cute" or "adorable"—or

any of the million other words
for someone attractive but not

attractive enough. "I need your help
cleaning up the edges," I said.

I took the guard off,
handing Hunter the shears.

I leaned over the sink, worried
what my mom would say, terrified

what Clown would say when he saw.
But not worried in the least

what Hunter would do.
"Wait," he said, "you missed a spot."

And I read his mind and said, "Wait!"
because there was no guard on the shears

and the second they touched my hair
they cut all the way to the scalp.

It didn't hurt or anything. I wasn't bleeding.
But Hunter said, "Fuck. Fuck!" and I knew

he couldn't fix it. I'd have to buzz my whole head
to the skin.

"I'm sorry," he said, and then his eyes welled up,
reminding me of our argument.

"Don't hate me," he begged, as if I could.
Suddenly I didn't care that I had a bald patch

two inches above my ear. I hugged him hard
as he cried harder. "Why am I so stupid?

Why do you even love me?" Hunter asked.
He sat on the edge of the tub, covering his face.

"You're not stupid," I told him, still in shock,
running my fingers over the missing chunk.

"You must love me a lot," I said,
"to want to make me ugly."

And Hunter laughed, crying harder, his nose running
on my shirt, on my neck.

"See," I said. "I'm funny, too."
And Hunter sobbed, nodding against me.

"I know you are," he said.
"But you couldn't be ugly."

PLATONIC

You call it love because it fits.
Look at my arm draped across you.
My head on your shoulder.
But what about the rest?

My mom says her friend saw us
together on the trail,
asked, was that my boyfriend?
Her friend said she couldn't tell,

that we could have just been
two guys walking together, platonically.
My mom sounded proud, or reassured,
said it was good to hear,

as if that vibe between us
might someday save us
if we're in the wrong place
at the wrong time. And it hurts to hear.

I tell her she's crazy, her friend.
That we're clearly a couple.
Except, why am I upset?
And why at her, and not you?

SELFLESS

I am pure energy   he is pure energy   our lips our tongues
the tips of our noses   I play at being a waterfall   turn all the
lights out   make believe he's here   under over in between
I lick the air   I paw the sheets   believing in a future   I pin
him in   nibble his knees   his nipples   even his eyelids   he
laughs as I   baste his back   with my sweat   our skin wet
our hair   my curls his   blond buzz   all of us   wet no
longer   wisps but rivers   give in to my   need I breathe
him in   through my mouth   through my eyes   I don't need to
see   to see him   his thin chest   his bright body   his
endless eyes   I'm always so close   to being a man   to
being his man   his answer   so close to being   eaten   by
eternity   my longed-for   ending   I bite my lip   pretend
it's him   pulling it   into his mouth   I switch hands   rub my
own   back my neck   moan my own name   making my voice
high as his   I beg myself   not to stop   never to stop   no
matter how   hard I grip   my own slick ankle   never leave
I say I need   never to be   apart after   I roll in place
grind my hips   so hard it hurts   sucking my own   tongue
sniffing my own   inner elbow   I crane my neck   let my skin
fold itself   into whatever shape   it takes   to feel something
I've never felt   so touched   as when he slid   his smooth
palm   up my leg   feel   my own heat   see   I hear him
ask   was it worth the wait   yes I say   a million times   yes
he's telling me   he loves me somehow   panting back
groaning   without words without   even being here   this
could be us   I say   faster   I say   always   this could be
all I need   is him   not to stop   loving me   my pulse   a
wreck   this could be   enough   oh   let it be   the last
time   I have to   be us both

HOPELESS ROMANTIC

Hunter and I are at the library,
me in Test Prep, him in Poetry.
When I find him, he has his finger
wedged between two books.
"This is where I'll be," he says.
And sure enough, he's in the Gs,
where his last name falls in the alphabet.
The shelf is full, and the space he's made
pinches the tip of his finger white.
I hug him from behind, amused
at his ability to believe in me.
"I'm ready," I tell him, but he says
he has to live there now, in the library.
"I can't leave," Hunter says.
"My spot needs me."
And I know it's a joke,
I know he's kidding,
but he's also not, somehow.
And I wonder,
is he as sure as I think he is?
Is he as sure as he lets on,
of his place on the shelf,
and of me, in charge
of our deliverance?
If so, good. I'm glad.
"I'm ready," I repeat,
afraid, knowing
he'll hold me
to it. And
this time
he hears
it, hears
me.

FIRST SEXT

1

No warning.
Just his naked waist, and lower.

I remember laughing, thinking it was all a joke.
Wanting it to be. Wanting it not to be.

Was that really him, really his?

But Hunter insisted he wasn't kidding.
Come on, he said. *I showed you mine.*

Then, *You said you were ready.*

I trusted him. That wasn't the problem.
He'd kept so many of our secrets
that I knew he wouldn't show anyone or tell.

And yet my hand shook, steadying my phone
to take the first picture. I took photo after photo,
but not sending them, none of them feeling right.

But it wasn't the pictures that were wrong.
It was the situation. I was aware, even then,
that once we started we might never stop.

Once he'd seen it, I could never again blush,
never again tell him it would be worth the wait.
He would have seen it and it would have become his.

I want to see you, Hunter texted,
as if he was angling to see my soul.
I want to see all of you. I love you.

He sent me another picture.
I closed my eyes, picturing him in bed with me,
imagining him beside me.

Please? Hunter said,
and I swallowed hard,
my mouth going dry.

I knew that once he saw mine,
he'd want to touch it.
He'd say, "What's the difference?"

and I'd have no answer.
After all, didn't I want him to touch it?
I wanted to explore the world with him, the universe.

Infinitely out. And
infinitely
in.

Promise? I asked him.
He sent me another, but of his naked chest and smiling face.
I could see the desire in his eyes.

He looked the same, but different.
As if he were looking through me, beyond our timeline,
at something already happening between us.

I could feel it in his gaze.
Electric. Eternal.
In some other universe

we'd already done everything
and seen everything
and loved what we'd seen.

Tell me you'll love me, even if I don't.
I waited a long time for him to write me back.
Too long. I wanted to go to sleep and pretend

none of our conversation had happened.
Of course I will, Hunter texted eventually.
But I also will if you do.

And those words were the key
to something I didn't know was locked.
I hadn't admitted it to myself.

I realized then
a part of me worried
sex might be the end.

I don't care if you're big,
Hunter texted. And I almost laughed.
It sounded like a challenge.

Not an issue, I replied.
My phone buzzed. It was him, calling.
When I answered, his voice seemed unfamiliar.

"Do you like mine?" Hunter asked me.
It hadn't occurred to me that he would question it.
Of course I did. It was his, after all.

And yet he sounded so vulnerable.
I was with him. I was there. All of me was.
"I love it," I told him. "I want to kiss it."

Hunter seemed to like that. He sounded
like he was going to cry suddenly, in a good way.
"I wish you were here," he said.

"I am," I insisted. But I knew what he meant.
"Fine," I said, and hung up.
I sent him a picture back, then called him.

"I love yours, too," he said as soon as he answered.
And then he thanked me.
And then he thanked me again, groaning.

"It doesn't change anything," Hunter said,
after it was over. "We're the same. See?"
But it wasn't true. I felt different.

The next day at school I could see it in his eyes.
He felt different, too. More, somehow.
And yet I wasn't worried.

We had a secret again.
A grown-up version of our first, closeted kiss.
I realized that I half expected Hunter

to make an ultimatum that night.
He was ready, after all. And if I wasn't,
maybe he would find someone who was.

But Hunter never said that.
I'm not sure if the thought even crossed his mind.
And so I felt closer to him than I ever thought possible.

MEANWHILE
(FROM THE OUTSIDE LOOKING IN)

WHAT IT'S LIKE WITH A COUPLE

All they have to say is "love"
and I swoon, a cut flower
going limp in water. Dammit.

What might I become if I were seen
as they see each other?

Sometimes I fear
I would disappear.
                              And so what?
I'm already a pink cloud contrail
dispersing on the air—
so much like skywriting,
yet desperately illegible.

Don't kid yourself.
I'm not as confused as I seem,
painting myself
a different color every morning.
Hoping someone will gag
for my so-so *eleganza.*
I'm simply pining.
Like everyone
but them.
These
two.

Dammit.

When I'm homesick, carrying
my heart full-o'-blood
with me like a duffel,
sometimes I stop

to lean over a railing.
Or lie on my chest
over the edge
and let my head dangle.
"Look down and spit,"
a voice inside me says.
But there are people down there,
so I don't. I never do.

I hold doors for old women,
even as their faces sour.
I say thank you at every kindness,
and hold it hard in my heart
amazed at how long gratitude can last
if you watch it carefully.
And when any couple walks up, any,
and their happiness is spread across them
like a blanket over two laps,
I tell the voice inside me
not to worry.
Not until
I give up.

I'm just waiting for that other self, outside me,
outside the borders of my affection's map,
who already knows me, accepts me.
Who dreams of my brown face and long, lustrous neck,
candy cigarettes powdering my lips—
who doesn't yet know
that I'm a real person to be found,
as real as they are.

"I'm not lonely," I tell my friends,
though no one said otherwise.

According to the calendar, it's only fall,
but nothing is to be believed.
I know what dead looks like.
The trees gave away

nearly all of their leaves.
And the few that are left
don't even know it.

I wish people were as easy to read
as nature.

"Maybe. Yeah," Hunter says
for them both.
And though they're just standing there,
in my head they're twirling, palm to palm.
"You're not fooling anyone,"
I want to say to Hunter
when he's all brood and sigh,
nothing seething inside.

"You love him so thoroughly
you don't even know what it's like
anymore, to not be loved back."

But talking to both of them,
I can't say anything.
Instead I purse my lips,
hoping one or both
know exactly what I mean.

A KISS IS JUST A KISS

Playing Spin the Bottle with Vanilla and Hunter
is like playing Capture the Flag.
Hunter wants the bottle—the boot—so badly
to stop on one of them,
while Vanilla wants the opposite.
Making each of them a target
on opposing sides of a circle.

And so The Gang and I take turns
trying to rig the game,
with Vanilla leaning away from the boot
and Hunter leaning into it
and everyone keeping score,
who's been kissed and who hasn't,
until it's only them left.

When I spin it, I hope it's Hunter,
and also hope so badly that it's not.
Wanting both
to kiss him, finally, and not to have to
kiss him now, like this,
when it's part of some game,
and I have to pretend not to like it.

Then it's Vanilla's turn to spin,
and The Gang leans in, watching the boot
slow and stop. Hunter leans in
because he feels he has to. And sure enough
he's won again. Only Hunter doesn't
seem to want the prize. Yet when they kiss,
it's more beautiful than I let myself imagine.

AFTER PARTY

"You be Hunter. I'll be Vanilla," I tell Abercrombie,
at our singles-only party, the morning after Halloween.

I beg him to seduce me,
doing my best impersonation of Vanilla's brand of innocence.

"I'm a poet," Ab says. "I work in rhythms!
Let me *read* all over you. Words! Words!"

Ab lifts his shirt and grinds the air. Marker still on his chest.
Already he's lost me. "Hunter wouldn't do that,"

I tell him. But he doesn't care.
"Vanilla wouldn't beg for it, either," Ab says,

and I realize I've forgotten who I am.
When I tell him to stop, he laughs.

"That's a good Vanilla," he says,
but I'm not playing anymore.

EARLY DAYS

Hunter invited himself over to "study"—
except we only had one class together
and it never had homework.
So I wondered what he was after.
Correction: I didn't wonder. I thought I knew.

I cleaned my room,
made my bed, imagining him
pulling back my sheets.

I tidied the bathroom,
hiding all of my products, wanting him
to find me beautiful all on my own.

I swept the kitchen, wiped the counters,
trying to see my house
through Hunter's eyes.

"What's gotten into you?"
my grandma asked. I hurried
to help her put groceries away,

not wanting Hunter to see
what childish shit I eat
when I'm not at school.

The doorbell rang, and I leapt to answer it.
And it was Hunter, of course.
No Vanilla in sight.

For a second I thought,
What are you doing?
But it isn't my job

to guard Vanilla's heart,
to put a fence around my own
with a sign: NO TRESPASSING.

All my life I've been the one
watching people fall in love.
I wanted it to be me this time,

no matter who else
may have gotten hurt
in the process.

But as I was thinking it,
Hunter was shaking my grandma's hand,
telling her, "No, we're just friends."

She looked at me with the same pity
she did when she first caught me
wearing her makeup,

as if to say, "I knew it
all along, what you've been doing.
And it isn't right."

DIAGRAMS

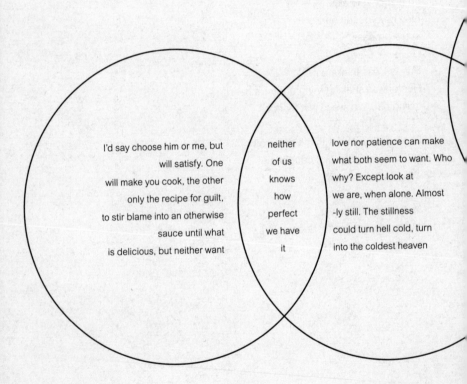

I'd say choose him or me, but
will satisfy. One
will make you cook, the other
only the recipe for guilt,
to stir blame into an otherwise
sauce until what
is delicious, but neither want

neither
of us
knows
how
perfect
we have
it

love nor patience can make
what both seem to want. Who
why? Except look at
we are, when alone. Almost
-ly still. The stillness
could turn hell cold, turn
into the coldest heaven

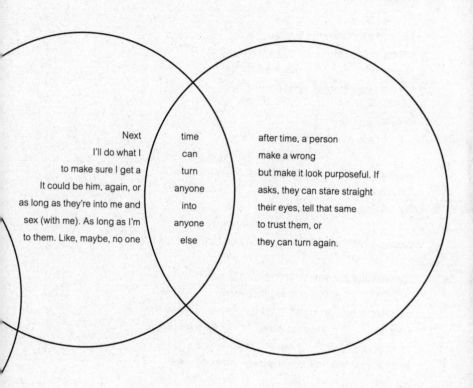

Next   time   after time, a person
I'll do what I   can   make a wrong
to make sure I get a   turn   but make it look purposeful. If
It could be him, again, or   anyone   asks, they can stare straight
as long as they're into me and   into   their eyes, tell that same
sex (with me). As long as I'm   anyone   to trust them, or
to them. Like, maybe, no one   else   they can turn again.

I WANT TO BE A POET TOO

I look in his eyes and it's music:
the muttering rap   of bridges half-sung
half-spoken.   a custom ringtone
the acknowledgment of a new friend.

Only he isn't new.
     I have a sea of need in me.
                         He is the tug of the moon
watering my tide   it swells with delay.
Offshore   storm.   He says
the waiting is excruciating,
                    and I wonder
Does he know what he's saying or who he's saying it to?

Can he hear himself or see inside my eyes?
              Another day, another year
watching them. And what does it mean   if I take him
take him in   in the meantime,   give him some
of what he craves.   These shadow touches
and the doublespeak   innuendo. Make him feel
wanted?   It isn't   guilt I feel   not exactly
looking at Vanilla's hands   as he cracks his knuckles.
It's   an ache
of self-knowing
              at his expense   though it costs him nothing.

Nothing.   Nothing.   Nothing.

As soon as Vanilla   comes around—if he   ever does—
he will have   not only his Hunter   but mine.   The Hunter
who texts after   midnight, test-driving   lines
for poems   half-written, asking
                         which version of the truth
is most beautiful. The Hunter   who sends photos
with his mouth wide open   asking

which sunglasses   make him look less desperate.
The   Hunter who waits   for everyone else   to stop listening
and then whispers   that I look pretty.

Even when the poems   aren't written for me
they make me blood-deaf   with jealousy.

I know there's room in Hunter's big heart for all of us.

And if one day   he hardens to waiting,   if whatever chamber
Vanilla has laid   claim to   calcifies,   with or without one of them
in it,   maybe   it will be my love   that saves Hunter,
keeps his whole heart   from becoming a fossil, a tomb.

And if not, what's the harm?

I look in his eyes, and it's music:
the muttering rap   of bridges sung
secrets never spoken,   a knowing   look.   Expecting

nothing   nothing   nothing   in return.

ONE FOR ME

Write *me* a poem.
I'll be whatever metaphor.
Make me the fastest animal.

I'll read it forever and never tell.
Unless you want me to.

HALLOWEEN

I'm afraid it's the Year of the Hunter,
the year I'm destined to have my heart broken.

      I love you like long-weathered wood.
      Like a piano without strings.

      Or like a piano with strings, but no keys, no hammers.
      Like a harp laid down to die in a box.

But you open that coffin, grinning, gentle,
a toy mallet in each hand. Ready to play.

Tell me the joke again, the one about Vanilla
losing his shit when I tell it like it is.

Tell me the one about Halloween night,
when he stormed out, afraid of what you'd do.

How he left and you saw and you stayed with me.
How I reached in your pocket and turned off your phone.

      I love you like a carousel.
      Like painted ponies moon-stepping

      up and down, with the kindest gravity.

Tell me the one where we danced, arm in arm,
spinning as fast as possible. Before the music even came back on.

Or the one where I turned your phone back on
as you passed out. Read Vanilla's texts, then fed you water.

      Sometimes, I think this could be enough.
      With or without momentum. With

or without you opening the box I'm in.
That I could lie here, happy, waiting

as long as it took. The sky is full, a flock of arrows.
They'll hit the ground eventually, here and there.

Pinning us each to ourselves, where we lie.
And maybe by then you'll be on top of me,

so we can be together when we're struck.

HIDING TOGETHER

Hunter has answers for everything.
Some make sense to me and others don't.
But it all makes sense to him, which is all that matters.

I tell him he's good at everything and he shakes his head.
"You only see me doing things I'm good at," he says,
calling it an accidental illusion.

I ask him what he's bad at,
but he refuses to answer.
I smile. (I smile a lot with Hunter.)

Doing homework together is funny. Because I have a huge paper to write,
and Hunter has only a poem. And yet we both seem to work as hard at it,
which seems insane.

He writes five poems, as if he's digging his way back to one.
And I want to ask what was wrong with the others,
but I don't want to interrupt him while he's working.

I want him to be finished
so I can pretend to be finished, too.
And listen to the poem Hunter wrote

while we were killing time together.

When Hunter's in a poetry mind-set
every answer sounds like a poem to me.
And in a way, every question does, too.

"Poetry must be hard," I say, and Hunter agrees.
His writing teacher has asked him to write a sonnet.
I ask what a sonnet is, expecting a definition.

"A sonnet is a sound, but petrified," he says.
Then he writes it down in his journal,
looking pleased with himself.

Vanilla texts Hunter, and I watch as he ignores it.
Then an hour later, Vanilla texts me,
explaining that Hunter gave him my number.
It feels wrong, but I ignore it, too. Following Hunter's lead.
And it feels wrong, what we're doing.
Though we never do anything.

Hunter says he feels blocked,
says he can't write and doesn't know why.
He takes me to the park,

to where he plays at being a gardener.
Hunter and his mom live in an apartment,
which doesn't have a yard. Instead, he comes here

and plants things off the beaten path, in secret.
I'm supposed to be working on my paper,
but I can't stop watching him, down on his knees,

digging and humming, like he does when he's writing.
His hands turning black, the harder he works,
until they're darker than mine.

I ask him why he doesn't plant things in Vanilla's yard,
and he says that he won't live there forever,
as if the park will never go away.

And then he thinks for a while,
wiping the sweat from his forehead with the white of his forearm.
I sit alone with my computer hot in my lap.

"Can you keep a secret?" he says,
and I want to say, "You have no idea."
Instead I nod, expecting something poetic.

But he waves me up, onto my feet with his dirty hands.
Then he leads me to a part of the park I've never been,
and shows me a tangle of vines he's been growing there, hidden.

He's tied fallen branches together, forming a kind of teepee,
and has trained vines to grow in a woven spiral around it,
so that the center is hollow, just big enough for two people.

I know it's not for me. That's why it's a secret.
But I can't help but picture myself
standing in Vanilla's place.

I'm usually so good
at appreciating what Vanilla can't,
but as I watch Hunter

work on their weird nest,
I find myself at a loss.
He can't stop touching the loose shoots,

forcing them into place,
and I can't stop
scratching my head.

There are plenty of places
to kiss, as is. Places with room
to spread out. To lie down together.

I want to ask him, "Why?
For what reason?" But the questions
feel wrong in my head,

until I feel
blocked, too. And instead
of asking why,

I ask him when,
knowing
he must have a plan.

"When it blooms again," he says. "Next summer, I guess."
And I picture the tent of vines, covered in flowers,
inebriating the air.

How could he possibly know
they'll be together then? Why not bring Vanilla now,
before it's too late?

The questions well up in my throat,
with nowhere to go. Until they spill out of me.
"Why?" I want to ask. But it comes out crooked.

"Why vines?" What I should have said is,
if you're going to spend time on something,
why this, why now, when you could do something that matters?

Hunter shrugs. "Why not?"
And I can tell I've hurt his feelings a little
by not being as impressed as usual.

Vanilla texts again, and this time Hunter responds.
I watch him write back, grinning at the screen,
his fingers still caked with dirt.

"I'm gonna go," he says.
I wish him luck.
I'm not sure why.

I wrote you a poem, Hunter texts later that night.
But he's too quick to correct himself.
I wrote a poem in response to what you said.

And I think, *What's the difference?*
And then I read it, and I know.

WHY VINES?

For Clown, Curer of Writer's Block

You can see who they are, their becoming.
Wherever there's space in the wild heart, they fill it.

The wood is still lightning green;
you can clip it with a fingernail.

But let it bloom a few times
and the bark will look rough to you.

I want all life I touch to flourish,
like a flower of myself. And of him.

But love moves outward. If it comes back at all,
it isn't the same love as what I sent.

Blooms are never inevitable.

Like one's human body,
a vine is not a static thing.

Instead, it is a manifestation
of many slow actions. Some conscious, most not.

And love is like that,
so a vine is like love.

But that isn't my real answer. Not if I'm honest.

Sometimes I want to go back to the beginning,
to when nothing had happened yet.

Hoping if we both went back, we'd feel
what it was like at first. I want to know finally

if what changed was us,
or something else. If time adds or subtracts,

or transforms only.
Or maybe it's that I wish I'd kissed him then,

right from the start
so that the two of us weren't friends first.

Thinking maybe it was a trap.

LOVE ME TENDER

When you reach for me, pretend it's your own skin,
your own small hairs being tickled.

Kiss my mouth like you know what it feels like
to be a tongue, surrounded by teeth and yet defenseless.

If you walk up behind me in the hall,
say my name *before* you put your arms around me,

as if you know what it feels like to be startled
by someone you love and yet inexplicably fear.

I want to hear your voice out of nowhere.
I want to know it's you whose hands start up my shirt.

Not only so I don't think it's someone else entirely.
But also so I can practice being loved comfortably.

> Without my skin crawling.
> Without hating it a little.

WHAT TRYING LOOKS LIKE

1

Hunter used to say he loved listening
to how I'd introduce us to strangers, that he loved
how I'd sum up our story. I'd call us "best friends
who like to kiss" or "boyfriends who happen
to be friends, too." And whichever it was,
we'd have a little laugh.
                                    But lately, Hunter
does the introductions. He calls us by our real names
and leaves it at that, as if he doesn't want anyone to know
we're a couple at all. "I feel like we're bragging," he says,
as if love itself were some kind of competition
we've won. Someone else's loss.
                                    "Besides," he says,
"we're more than friends." And I agree,
even though I don't. Feeling suddenly like I've lost a best friend
in a negotiation I didn't know we were having.

2

Hunter used to lie next to me on the couch,
with his arm around my waist. Sometimes,
without thinking, he'd brush my side with his thumb,
grazing my rib cage as we watched TV. "That tickles,"
I'd say, and he'd quit. Only to start again, moments later.
"You're tickling me!" I'd tell him, grabbing his hand.
"I'm sorry," he'd say, "I'll stop." But I didn't want him to stop.
It only tickled when he did it too hard or too soft.
"I like it," I said, "when you do it right."

3

Hunter shows me The Gang's invite,
tells me Abercrombie wants me there.
"I thought I embarrassed you last time," I say,
and he tells me we were drunk,
as if we both were,
as if we're both forgiven.
"You can go," I say.
"Do you really want me there?"
I prepare myself for his hesitation,
fearing what he secretly wants
is to go alone.
"I don't want to go without you," he tells me.
"But I do want to go."

4

Hunter found an app
that syncs a folder in our phones
so that I can see a saved sext from him
whenever I want and
he can see mine.
Needless to say,
my penis is outnumbered
three to one at least.
"It isn't that I'm not horny,"
I promise him. "All those
dicks are as sexy as it gets."
And yet, it never seems enough.
I don't moan loud or dirty,
don't get into it fully,
in part because I don't want him
able to say later that
what we're doing already
is sex. That we're having sex already,
only apart. Which is how
I maybe feel, in the moment,

the times I let my guard down
and show a little bit of my face.

5

Hunter brings over his laptop
before my mom gets home.
At first we're doing homework,
but without warning, he says he needs to
"clear his mind,"
opening a new page,
pulling up porn.

He watches the screen, seeming to believe
those bodies are real. I watch the color change
on his cheeks. And when it does, I hurry to look,
to see what exactly
has made him flush—
or is it only their reflections,
someone's skin cast over his?
I watch his eyes, fixed
like fastened stars, his pupils
seeming never to move.
Though sometimes
the skin under his eyes tenses,
and I can tell he's thinking.
I glance back at the screen,
afraid to look, afraid to see
something I might be made to do.

I see men splayed naked, kissing
or having sex or both,
and when Hunter checks,
I fake it: letting my face
go dumb as his
until his eyes
are off me.

The first clip ends, and he asks
if another's okay. And I agree, grateful
it's still those bodies he wants
instead of mine.

6

Hunter comes back from the bathroom,
fly zipped and hands dry.
I blush as he grins, not meeting my gaze.
He flops onto my bed, beside me.
I want nothing more than to curl up against him,
to feel his pulse as it slows, as he sleeps.
But I don't dare reach for him, afraid I haven't earned it.

That's when I feel Hunter's hand grab mine.
He squeezes it so hard, I think he's saying something.
He puts his head on my shoulder, turns in place
until his body settles soft against mine,
forming a line of heat from his chest to his ankles.
His groin soft against my thigh, but still grinding.
I grind back, barely moving. Feeling Hunter
in the pace of it. Feeling his fall as he comes down.

This part I could like, I think. *I could look forward to this.*
Just as I'm thinking it, Hunter coughs
like he's clearing his throat to speak. His whole body
sighs and stills, even his groin.
"Thank you," he says. And I don't understand.
But I take it anyway and hold it so hard.
His hand still clutching mine.

WHAT TRYING LOOKS LIKE

The next time we're at party,
there's someone there we haven't met,
and Vanilla lets me introduce us however I want.

I tell our story like this:
After telling the dude our names,
I say, "We were so good at being friends,

we decided to be boyfriends." Vanilla takes my hand
and wraps it around his waist. I creep my thumb
up his side, stroking his rib cage under his shirt

with just the right amount of pressure.
"I want to be in love like that," the guy says,
looking around the room. Neither Vanilla nor I say it

but I know we're both thinking it:
There is no other love
like ours.

SELFLESS

I wake up and I'm hard,
so I send a picture to Hunter, as promised,
wondering if he can tell
if my heart's really in it.

He writes back, asking for a video.
Let's do it together, he tells me.
And I try to stay hard, thinking of how I do it
when it's just me, and it's not sex
but something else.

Every impulse bends inward
until I'm high on the charge,
able to aim those feelings
and explode myself
at will.

There's a build and a climax, and then release.
And with it, such a sweet loss of self
that I can wholeheartedly deny anything
in the moment. Including who I am,
what it is I'm doing. I disappear.

But the moment I think of Hunter or anyone,
it's not about me, not about my own feelings.
The moment of privacy
bursts like a soap bubble
inside me.

With Hunter, it's as if
his build depends on someone else's, on mine.
As if that same bubble inside him
might be shared between us both.
As if our bodies might read each other
the way our minds sometimes seem to.

I can imagine it like that with Hunter.
Sometimes, testing my limits,
I imagine Hunter's hand instead of my own
the very moment I'm to come undone.
And it doesn't always ruin it.

Sometimes, thinking about Hunter during,
I can conjure him next to me, share my escape.
And when it works, I'll grab my phone,
knowing how happy it will make him,
seeing it for himself.

I wish I could say it adds only.
Instead, it feels like being watched,
or like I'm lying to myself—which I am, I guess.
Mind over matter. And that fact makes me feel guilty.
Even if it's for Hunter's benefit.

NOCTURNAL

Wet ink glitters
in lamplight.
    It is yet another fact
    of midnight.
        Another being
        my tired mind
            aching to give
            itself a break.
During which time
a mindless body roves
    perfectly in place,
    as set ink, dried.
        Whitman was sleepless.
        Wandered slowly the streets,
            peering into parked carriages,
            hoping to spot a couple
or some solitary man,
his hardness hidden in shadow.
    Lowell, too—the man one,
    Catholic—watched for love-cars
        in "Skunk Hour"—
        More proper than Whitman
            his confession of "one dark night"
            stood, probably, for many.
He struck out, traipsing
through a dark
    New England town. His shame
    a borderless silence.
        "My mind's not right,"
        he wrote. Reading it,
            it seems as unpolished
            as a found knife carried
under one's cloak,
pulled out to startle

a nun. Or me,
browsing shameless.
Only unlike Whitman
or Lowell, I stay put,
wandering past pages
instead of porches,
never leaving my room.
Still, I'm that young man
wearing danger
like a trench coat,
giving strangers
false names
and falser hopes.
Every erection
seemed a statue once.
Momentary god
having earned someone's worship.
Now I beg for strangers' trust
only to betray them
with silence.
My spoils are headless torsos,
Elysian only at first glance.
I forgive them
for their shadow contours,
cropped angles,
tricks of light.
In fact, I thank them
moaning with boyish gratitude,
unriddling each man
by his chin . . .
A person in love
doesn't hide
unless weeping in his car.
Doesn't roam anonymous,
a phantom of eyes,
slippery to consequence.
Whitman would be queer
in any age. Lowell was

a puritanical prude,
married three times and in love
      with his lesbian bff.
      What's my excuse?
          It was one thing
          when I was against a wall.
              Now it's another.
              Each direction
                    the devil flies
                    is Hell.
Not even a Catholic,
I know that.
      I myself
      the arrow
          of a wind vane,
          squealing for a storm.
              North, northeast,
              then suddenly south.
Like a cat
on a fence
      in silhouette.
      Or the fence itself,
          dark below dark,
          sealing the family in.

STRANGER DANGER (AMUSE-BOUCHE)

I toss a made-up name in a stranger's inbox,
pay some guy an empty compliment,
and for the next two hours
we're fast friends, flirting
in the mind's darkest alley.

I feel like a shape-shifter,
telling each new man a different lie.
A fact-finding mission, to see
which disguise
is most appetizing.

I tell myself it isn't cheating,
because it isn't about getting off, for the most part.
I don't need anyone else for that,
not with my wild imagination.
Not with Vanilla warming up to the idea.

But it's fun to tug from one end of a line
and feel someone there who wants it.
Problem is, what do I do
when I've caught something,
and it's on its back, my mouth at its throat?

It's one thing to practice being cocky and sure,
another not to notice when a person
puts his heart in the ring.
Or to not show up when it finally matters.
Ruining someone's night. My own make-believe.

Sometimes, if it's late, and the walls I put up
are giving out, the bricks I stacked
turn back into pumpkins
and tumble down.
Suddenly it feels good to tell the truth, any of it.

Vulnerability's skin
drawn, made flush
by a solidarity for pleasure.
Familiar and pure
as it is at its best with Vanilla.

Except before I know it, I can start to care
who the guy really is. What it might be like
to stop bluffing and follow the bread-crumb trail
hungry to his door. It makes me realize
just how starved I am.

Able to spot in the snow a single seed
of true affection. Knowing and not knowing
what it might become
without the mistake of going slow.
Without worrying too soon about consequences.

And sometimes a guy won't take no for an answer,
and when I go quiet, he pulls me back.
I'm dizzy now, aware of the bends.
He'll let down his guard,
tell me his real name.

He asks why I'm cheating, and I insist I'm not.
He asks why not, and I say I love my boyfriend.
Writing the words, I wonder
what he must think of me. If I led him on.
And if he understands. If anyone could.

I see he's typing. Then I see he's not.
For a long while, nothing.
Until it's the waiting, not the joy, that feels familiar,
and my mind translates new loneliness
from the old, circling back like destiny.

I tell him I should go, and he asks me why.
And I tell him because I'm worried what I'll do,
which is the last thing I should say, I know,

because if it were Vanilla who said that,
it would be my cue to come on strong.

I'm proud of you, he writes,
as if I should be proud of myself.
But instead, as I fold the screen down,
the darkness of the room
throbs in my skull.

I lie back on my bed,
lie motionless, listening
to the sound of my chest,
my body still galloping in place.
And there in that stillness,

I realize it will never feel enough.
Even when I'm spent, I never feel emptied.
Never feel fuller than when I started.
Instead, it's like I want to be reminded endlessly
of what I already have, what I already know.

THE LETTER

Freshman year, Red and I would fight
and it would get so bad my mom would intervene.
"You can't keep hanging out with her," she'd say.
"Not if you two can't dial it down a notch."

Dad taught me to write my feelings down.
Put it all in a letter, even if I never send it.
I did, and it worked. And I've done it ever since.
Not only with Red, but with everyone.

Once, instead of a fight with Hunter,
I poured my heart out longhand.
For three pages, I ranted in ballpoint scrawl.
And at the end of it, I decided
the fight wasn't worth it.
I put the letter in a drawer.

A year went by, and I forgot all about it.
Until Hunter was helping me clean
and found it there, addressed to him,
full of complaints I only half meant.
Luckily, he understood, since he's a writer
and has written his own half-truths.

Ever since, I type my letters out,
putting my thoughts down in a blank document.
And always—almost always—I trash it.
I say *almost* because there's one I didn't delete.
Writing it felt different. In every way.
Probably because it's addressed to myself.
Saved on my desktop, where I return to it
nightly now. Reading the last few paragraphs
over and over. Trying to figure out what I meant.

I was exhausted when I wrote it. Sad and angry.
But I remember typing those words, thinking,
*Don't you disregard yourself, don't dare read this later
and shrug it off. You're finally saying what you mean,
so hear it.* Seeing the words again, I cried.
And seeing them now, I'm all cried out.

What do I mean, I wish there was no such thing
as sex? What do I mean when I tell myself
I can't give Hunter what he wants after all?
Because I *can*. And what did I mean when I said
I was glad I'm ugly, because it makes me trust
that Hunter's not a perv like Abercrombie or Clown,
drooling over bodies like my boyfriend's body.
I don't really think I'm ugly, so what was I after?

I read the whole thing over, from the beginning,
looking for clues, trying to remember that night.
I don't feel broken, like something's wrong with me.
What did I mean by the word *boring*,
when I described that scene in the movie
that made the rest of The Gang go quiet?
And how did they know which parts were funny
and which were just weird? Because it all seemed
weird to me.
It's like something's wrong with everyone else.
Yet it's me that blushes first, blushes most.

For the past three nights, I've reread my letter.
It's the last thing I do before going to sleep.
Even on nights we play Hunter's game until late,
and he finishes, and I play along.
Hunter will fall asleep, still on the line.
And no matter how sleepy I am,
I pull out my laptop and add a few paragraphs.
If I don't, I can't sleep.

Strangely, the writing is harder
now that I know I'll read it again.

It's not until I convince myself
I'm not journaling or confessing anything
that I start to say what I really mean.
And only then do I feel okay again,
trusting myself with my secrets.

I'll tilt the screen down all but an inch,
and leave some music playing.
I'll roll onto my side, away from its light.
I don't know why I feel better
knowing the letter's there, awake while I'm sleeping.
But I do.

SEX TALK

Clown asks if I'm a top or a bottom,
and when I say I'm neither,
he laughs.
"I know," he says.
"But if you got any,
which would you get?"

And I tell him I'm not sure,
because it seems like the luck of the draw
and I'd happily take or give
whatever Vanilla wanted
as long as he wanted it
and wanted me.

Clown asks if he's big, like it matters.
And I tell him he's perfect in every way,
forgetting that I wasn't supposed to tell.
Clown asks if I have a picture,
And I lie and tell him I deleted it.

"You're a top," he says.
"I can always tell."
And I let him think it,
even if it means
he might repeat it
to Vanilla.

Because at least Clown
sees me as sexual,
can imagine me
on top of someone.
While Vanilla seems to hate
imagining me in any position.

TWO-FACED

Have you ever made a fake profile?
Ever bared yourself to the universe,
and for all eternity, throwing
caution to the wind and
sheets over furniture
so no one would
recognize your
boyhood bed?

Have you ever lied to your boyfriend
and said you weren't mad anymore,
simply to avoid having to confront him,
or, worse, comfort him?

Have you ever slinked away
from your snakeskin, thinking
you can crawl back at any time—
only to find your old body
no longer fits and you don't know
anymore what it is you want?

Have you ever flirted with a friend
you're not even attracted to?
Or become attracted to a friend
you never would have guessed
could make you feel more yourself
at the exact moment you needed it?

Have you led someone on
by accident? Holding on to them
too long, too hard? Meaning it
too much?

Have you ever wished
on a porn star,

wishing
wishes were real, knowing
they're not?

Have you ever lied to the person you love,
said you could wait, when you knew you couldn't?

Have you ever taken a train
in the middle of the night, not knowing where you're going,
only to end up in the next state, your eyes so dry
you could barely keep them open,
then waited on the cold platform
for the next train back?

Have you ever posted pictures of yourself,
curious who, if anyone, would want you?
No face, no incriminating details,
just body parts
that could belong
to anyone?

Have you ever posted a picture of the person you love
to see who else could love him?

And then
did you wait
for someone—
anyone—
to notice?

CRUSH

Vanilla and I used to play this game we called Crush.
We took turns confessing who we thought was cute,
followed, of course, by a lovestruck litany of reasons
we would never want anything outside each other.

He had only just begun to call me "boyfriend" back.
I'd been calling him it for weeks. To him, to friends,
and to my mom. Though she kept calling him
"first boyfriend"—as if there were bound to be more.

"Abe Lincoln," I'd say, feigning a swoon. And Vanilla
would cross his arms and put on a pouty frown,
as if who *I* have a crush on somehow reflects on *him*.
As if my having a crush on Vanilla

and also having a crush on Person X therefore equals
Vanilla having a crush on anyone, ever. Or feeling anything,
other than what he doesn't want. Other than what he's decided
not to want. Like me, in my car, in a kind of preemptive exile.

Have you ever felt guilty?
And then felt guilty for feeling it?
As if you had promised yourself you wouldn't feel?
As if you aimed to be only a body,
without a soul?

I tried playing Crush with Vanilla again.
Yesterday, after school, I asked him,
"Hey, remember that game we used to play?"
Vanilla rolled his eyes.
"You mean the one where you told me who was cuter than me?
And then, when it was my turn, you wouldn't let me answer?
Fun game."

"That's not true," I said. At least, it's not how I remember playing.
Though as soon as Vanilla said it, a memory surfaced
of me tickling him so hard he couldn't breathe, purely to keep him
from answering.

"Well," I said, changing the subject, except not really,
"do you want to play now? I'll let you answer."

"No," Vanilla said.
"Besides, I already know who you have a crush on."

"But I don't know your crush," I said, and he blushed, said,
"Of course you do."

Have you ever felt like a monster?

Have you ever opened your email, having forgotten what you'd
    done,
and found too many messages, dripping with adoration?
Have you read them all, right there in a sitting, your door locked,
your fly open? Have you not lost your mind a little, in the moment?

Have you not taken in the sight of a site
all lit up with what you want
and basked in its flickering light,
forgiving yourself
and finally feeling
nothing?

Vanilla, if you're listening,
put a shield around your heart.

LIP SERVICE

I like meeting new people
because they ask questions.
      If I make a new friend,
      he or she will ask about me.
      And I'll tell them all about Vanilla,
      and all his favorite things.
If I ask what they think of him,
they'll answer, repeating everything I've said.
      Returning Vanilla to me,
      exactly as he was given.
But old friends don't ask questions.
Friends like Clown who already know me
      will never fully understand Vanilla.
      Clown cuts me off when he asks how I am
      and I try to tell him a story
      he thinks he's heard already.
Lately, the only way to get his attention
is to confess something, surprise him.
      He wants to think it's a new story this time,
      one in which he can help me find the ending.
"What if it isn't love I feel for Vanilla?" I ask,
fully believing I know how Clown *should* answer.
      Instead, he changes the subject,
      leaves what I've just said
      dangling there,
      dangerous.
"Ab's parents canceled their trip," he says.
"No party this weekend, I guess."
      I tell him my mom will be gone till Sunday,
      that he could move the party to my place if he wants.
"You're not serious," Clown says, like he knows better.
It's the reaction I wanted before. I guess that's why I insist.
      "You heard me," I say, as if
      I've never made a joke before in my life.

SECOND ULTIMATUM

1

I'm scrolling through Clown's feed
when Vanilla . . .

I'm laughing at Clown's draft invite
when Vanilla . . .

I'm texting Clown, *Nothing, just
reading. Why? What's up?*
when Vanilla . . .

2

I used to calm Vanilla down,
promising to warn him
if I ever wanted to cheat.

Now I want to rile him up.
I say, "This is that warning,"
and "I'm serious this time."

It's gotten to the point
that I fantasize more about snapping
than about not having to.

Vanilla crisscrosses his legs
and looks down into his notebook.

He nods his head. "I know," he says.
And, "It's okay." And, "I wouldn't blame you."

It breaks my heart to think he's as serious
as I am, that he's so afraid of sex
that he'd toss our love to the wolves.

3

It's about time I showed The Gang
who I really am, flying solo.
It's not like I'd be cheating, exactly.

But I'd definitely get flirted with, maybe groped.
Those guys are always pulling some prank,

putting their dicks in something.
And it would be hot to be there when they did it.

Show Clown and all of them
that I can be fun.

4

When Clown texts, *What's up?*
I write, *My dick.*

He eggs me on
until I'm not sure what's a joke and what isn't.

And yet, it's Clown who stops me, in the end.
Does Vanilla know you say shit like that?

And my silence says it all. *Good night, Huntress.*
And then nothing. His silence is longer than mine, says more.

What if there was no Vanilla? I type.
Pressing send hurts. It feels final,

regardless of Clown's reply. But he's like,
What if they sold McDonald's in the cafeteria?

I still wouldn't eat it.
And then my screen shows that he's typing something else.

You and I both know you'd eat this, I tell him,
wishing he'd admit it so we could both get some sleep.

I'm on a diet, he says. *Besides,*
I couldn't do that to someone.

I tell Clown I wish I could tell Vanilla what he said.
So he'd know Clown wouldn't hurt him.

And then it looks like Clown's typing.
And then it looks like he's not.

I didn't mean Vanilla, Clown finally tells me.
I couldn't do that to you.

PRE-PARTY

1

Red asks why I'm hanging out with Clown instead of her,
and I tell her it's not up to me. It's Hunter's party.
She asks why I have no say, and I tell her,
"Nothing's up to me anymore."

Red asks if she should come over, and I say, "I don't deserve it."
She thinks I mean that I don't deserve *her*,
her bothering to care after being taken for granted.

I don't tell her I mean Hunter's ticking clock,
his sniffing around for a Plan B boyfriend.
I don't deserve to be held at arm's length,
as if it's me who's halfway out the door.

"Yeah, you do," she says,
and she kisses me through the phone.
But all I hear is
Tick tick tick tick tick.

2

"I thought you said you'd never
go to one of their parties again,"
Hunter tells me,
as if he doesn't want me there.

"You got so mad after movie night," he goes on.
But I wasn't mad. I was quiet.
Unlike now, when I'm both.

"I know you'll be hosting," I say. "Don't worry.
I'm not going to follow you around like a puppy."
Hunter looks at me finally.

"Maybe Red can come and keep me company," I say.
"But if Red's invited, I have to invite all the girls," he replies.
"It's going to be way too crowded as is."

I hear Hunter's nerves. The pinch in his voice as he says it.
"You know I'm happy to help, right?" I ask.

But from the way he hugs me,
I guess he didn't know.

REASONING

I'm afraid
he'll notice
I've run out
of reasons

that what I
want no
longer aligns
with thought

that no
mind can
speak for the
both of me

(he should need
only to press
into me to
impress me)

No I still
say but
what I want
to say is

I know
I no
longer
make sense

PARTY AT HUNTER'S

1. *Stoli Wild Cherri*

It was promised to be one of those parties
no one talks about after.
But it was us this time—ours.

Clown kept saying, "I can't believe this is happening."
And Hunter kept saying, "I can't believe
it's taken me this long to host." Red kept texting
that she couldn't believe she wasn't invited,
and I kept
silent, nervous about what people were thinking,
and if Hunter would get caught.

Hunter said I needed a "co-host drink,"
so we went to the kitchen, where the bottles
were lined up, glass and labels of every color.
I didn't know what any of them were.

"Suicide?" Clown said, and he started pouring.
One second of this, four seconds of that
until I lost track of his recipe for daring.
"Maybe I shouldn't," I said. They already knew
I was thinking it. Hunter smiled,
pouring the potion from one cup to another,
back and forth, back and forth.
I realized I wanted to stay forever
in that moment, before anything else happened.
The two of us like those plastic cups,
and whatever was still sweet between us
pouring like infinity back and forth, his and mine.
I looked Hunter in the eyes and saw everything.
Back and forth, our love poured
from his eyes to mine and back.

There was nothing dangerous about the glimmer in his eyes.
No test. No bait. No poison.
Only him and me,
and the sound of the purple drink he was mixing
that sounded like the ocean
and the call and response of compliments.
Or like the babbling of two lovers:
"I love you." "I know."
"I need you." "I know."

But Clown had the cups and was dropping
fistfuls of ice into each, so loud
it almost made me laugh. I shook my head at him.
Then Hunter poured our concoction three ways, over the ice,
and time started again, my ticking clock.
I love him. He knows.
I need him. He knows.

Clown said, "Cheers," and we all clinked plastic.
Then he said, "Let the games begin."

2. *Bazooka Hooch*

Somewhere between Spin the Bottle and Seven Minutes in Heaven,
Abercrombie blew his lifeguard whistle and shouted, "Mixer Emergency!"
Everyone but me seemed to know what that meant.
I followed the herd to the kitchen, where a half-dozen half-naked boys
were raiding the pantry and fridge, searching for whatever they could find.
Powdered energy drinks, chocolate syrup, the dregs of strawberry jelly.
They argued over what was good-disgusting and what was bad.
A new game had started, in which everyone still standing
had to make a cocktail incorporating something from the mess.
Abercrombie kicked it off, mixing pickle juice and bourbon,
which he garnished with a Slim Jim (the rule was three ingredients,
    minimum).
Ab's boyfriend poured gin in the jelly jar and shook it up,
his pecs and biceps flexing, putting on a show.
He added some Skittles, which sank to the bottom and turned white.
A few guys chickened out, which meant they "lost" the game,

which meant they had to do a dare, which meant they each got more
  naked.
Clown's friend Kit from out of town, who no one seemed to know,
mixed a little bit of everything, from mustard and mayo to rum and tonic,
and we all chanted his name as we watched it curdle.
Hunter dunked a donut in Baileys and milk and everyone booed him.
And then it was my turn. I scanned the counter, not knowing what to do.
There were oatmeal packets and cans of chili, and my stomach turned
at the thought of drinking something that already looked like puke.
I realized I'd rather drink straight alcohol than mix in something chunky.
So I surprised everyone, pouring straight vodka over bubble gum,
and sprinkling it with cinnamon. Clown said, "Good one."
Then it was his turn. He took his sweet-ass time, too,
melting Life Savers into water in the microwave.
We weren't allowed to drink until everyone had a cocktail in hand.
Hunter's donut was soggy by then, and my inch and a half of vodka
had turned princess pink. Clown poured his purple-brown syrup
into Jäger and Coke, and everyone gagged as it fizzed.
Then everyone took a sip, even Kit,
and some of us groaned how gross it was, and some of us nodded,
proud of our inventions. Abercrombie blew his whistle,
and everyone passed their drink to the right. Some called foul
and some thanked heaven, finally able to get whatever taste out of their
  mouths.
We all took a second sip, laughing at Clown, who had Kit's cup.
"This is pretty good," Hunter said, finishing my bubble-gum vodka.
"So is this," I said, downing Clown's, which was more sweet than gross,
though it tasted a little like medicine. "We should mix," Hunter said,
and I thought he meant we should talk to strangers. But he meant the
  drinks.
"Too late for that," I said, holding my cup upside down. "No it isn't."
And then he pulled me in, in front of everyone, and kissed me hard.
The sweet on his tongue mixing with mine. I blushed but didn't stop
  myself,
loving how much he loved the attention. And when I looked up,
everyone was smiling at us like we'd won the game.

3. *Water*

I forget how they paired us up, but they did.
"No couples allowed," Clown said,
and he pulled Hunter and me apart.

I watched Hunter's eyes
to see who my boyfriend hoped would be his.
But he was blushing, looking into his drink.

And first it was Ab and Kit, then it was
two of the naked boys. Each pair
got locked in the closet for what seemed

like a small eternity. "I forgot my drink!"
Ab's boyfriend cried, his muffled voice
coming from behind the door,

but they wouldn't let him out.
"Drink his spit!" Ab yelled back,
and everyone laughed but me.

When the door opened, they were caught
making out hard. They squinted at us all,
only a little embarrassed. Both aroused

and proud of it. I searched Abercrombie's face,
but he was in on it. I searched Hunter's,
and he was, too. Scanning their bodies

and crotches, as I briefly had. His neck flushing
as he wiped his mouth. "Vanilla, you're up,"
Ab said, and then he said the other name.

It was Clown, and everyone laughed
the same as they'd laughed at the others.
I looked at Hunter to see if he was sad.

I think he was, but I wasn't sure
who for. Clown wrapped a boa around me,
and pulled me with him into the closet,

as my mouth went dry and I started sweating.
Imagining the conversations later
between Hunter and me,

because if I kissed Clown, why couldn't he?
So what if it was only a game?
So what if it was only seven minutes?

The door closed behind us, and
Clown stopped laughing. We listened
as they laughed at us, as they teased us both.

Clown offered me some of his drink
and I refused. "It's only water," he said,
but I didn't believe him. "Seriously," he said,

"you should have some water."
But I didn't understand. I was too busy
listening for Hunter's voice. "Don't worry,"

Clown said. "I'm not going to kiss you."
I asked him why, and he said
because he knew I didn't want to.

I told him I was sorry, and asked,
"Is that okay?" I think he nodded,
but my eyes were still adjusting,

having stared down at the bright
line of light at our feet until right then.
"Are you having fun?" Clown whispered

and I realized I was. "Yeah," I said,
looking at the shelf of clutter
behind Clown, remembering it was Hunter's

or Hunter's mother's, and realizing
I'd never seen any of it before.
Unsure whether to be humbled by it.

"You throw good parties," I said,
even though it was Hunter's apartment,
because it was Clown people had come for.

"Thanks," he said,
and then he added that the trick was
inviting cool people. I smiled,

hoping he could see it. Hoping
he meant me, too, and not only Hunter.
But why would he say it otherwise?

I drank Clown's water, wondering
if I should kiss him. "I'm sorry
I'm so predictable," I said, kissing him

on the cheek. "You're not," he promised.
And then he kissed my cheek back slow,
making sure to get a little lipstick on me.

"I do have a reputation to uphold," he said.
And then he took off his shirt
and I smiled, taking off mine.

Both of us laughed.
"Hunter's gonna freak,"
I said. And Clown asked why.

"Maybe he isn't," I said.
And we both got quiet.
Clown kissed me on the cheek again,

said, "They're gonna want to catch us."
So we mimed like we were making out,
though only our legs were touching.

I could feel Clown's breath on my skin,
could feel the heat between our bodies.
I could kiss him right now, I thought.

If everyone's going to think we did it anyway,
what's the difference? And so I inched
my body closer, until our naked chests

were barely touching. I licked my lips,
let the cup of ice fall to the floor.
Everyone was listening, I realized,

because they laughed at the sound it made.
And Clown let out a little sigh—or was
it more?—as I put my mouth behind his ear.

He nuzzled the back of my buzzed head
as he reached around my waist,
pulling me tighter. I surprised myself, getting into it,

then noticed he was, too. "You're good at pretending,"
he said. And I nodded, not wanting him
to stop. "Hunter *is* gonna freak,"

he repeated, as if it were a warning.
"Let him," I said. "It's just a game."
Clown pressed into me,

kissing my lips, our mouths closed,
like it was only about the lipstick.
But I could feel him

on the other side of it, his lips
parting ever so slightly. I ran my hand
where his bangs would be,

where I was used to fingering
Hunter's curls. And it felt good,
the difference. Every inch of Clown

a surprise. And as the door opened,
Clown pulled back. But I didn't—
I'm not sure why. In fact, I pulled him in

for one last kiss. And opened my mouth,
everyone cheering. Clown
laughed hard,

pushing me off of him
like it had all meant nothing,
which I guess it hadn't.

4. *Beer Run*

I thought the party was winding down.
There were only six people left, surrounded by empties.
We sat in a circle in Hunter's living room, telling stories.
It had been a game at first: listing things we hadn't done.
And those of us who had were forced to drink.
"It's the perfect game for you," Clown said, winking,
and for the first time I felt like I was allowed to laugh at the joke.
Eventually the game devolved from taking even turns,
to Abercrombie and Kit one-upping each other
while the rest of us listened, in awe of their exhibitionism.
Ab had made out with a postal worker, or so he claimed.
Kit had kissed a teacher, though none of us believed him.
"Which teachers would you kiss?" Hunter asked,
and each of us had to name at least one.
Some chose the obvious ones, the least old, least ugly,
and some made jokes about kissing Mr. Neardy—
who they called Nerdy—and how he'd taste like his inhaler.
Then Clown said he would kiss Mrs. Wright, and everyone agreed
not only that she was the hottest, but that Clown would totally kiss her.
He blushed, and we laughed, and he blushed some more.

For a moment it seemed like the party was over.
Hunter and I exchanged a familiar glance, nodding that it was time.
But I could tell neither of us wanted the night to end.
And then, as if we'd willed our own fate, the doorbell rang.

It was Ab's boyfriend again, and he'd brought back "boys and beer."
"Welcome," Clown said, putting his arm around the shyest one.
We played a new game, Old vs. New,
in which those of us who were already tipsy
got to tell the newbies what to do.

Hunter and I picked our favorite. We named him Boo.
He helped us clean up, carrying the trash bag behind us
throughout the house. When the place was clean, or at least cleared,
the three of us went to Hunter's room and closed the door.
We sat at the foot of his bed, whistling with our bottles.
Hunter was the best at it. I couldn't take my eyes off the shape of his lips.
Boo started whistling in harmony, without the bottle,
and I joined in, or tried to, knowing nothing about music.
The three of us sounded good together, I think,
and when Boo said as much, Hunter agreed.

I pulled the cord on my hoodie, so that I had no face,
only a nose and a top lip poking through the hole.
Then I wiggled my head out again,
bleary eyed as a newborn baby.
"Where do you go to school?" I asked,
but Boo said he didn't. He'd dropped out.
Hunter looked sad for him. And I felt happy,
knowing I might never see him again.
"How do you know Chuck?" Hunter asked,
and Boo said he didn't. That they'd met buying the beer.
And then Boo rolled a cigarette and almost lit it
before Hunter said he'd have to go down to the street.

"Whose place is this anyway?" Boo said, looking around,
and Hunter pretended not to know
as Boo started touching the stuff on his dresser.
"Cigarette?" Hunter said, reminding Boo,
and like a robot reminded of its mission,
he went for the door, and we followed him.
Back through the party and out to the street.
Clown came out and said Boo's ride was leaving,
and Boo waved his cigarette, as if it were

a unit of time. He looked at Hunter, then at me.
And when we didn't offer him a ride, he nodded.

I can't describe what it felt like, exactly.
Like winning, I guess. But with all the joy gone.
None of the three of us had anything to say suddenly.
But we hugged Boo—I'm not sure why.
Clown thanked him for helping clean up.
And then the party really was over.
At least, the part where we were all together.
Clown slept on the sofa bed, and Hunter and I
spooned in his room as the sun came up,
whistling in quiet harmony. "That was fun," he said,
and I agreed. He wiped Clown's lipstick off my neck,

telling me he was proud of me.
And I almost told him I was proud of me, too,
but the sun was making me sick inside,
and it didn't feel like we were playing anymore.

WHAT IT'S LIKE WITH MY FAMILY

With her husband out of earshot, Grandma asks if I'm dating.
She knows I'm not, but fishes anyway.
I catch her clocking my chipped nail polish,
my pierced ears, my eyeliner. "Nooope," I say.

"Well, I hope when you do, I'll get to meet him."
I know my heart should swell in my chest;
it's a kind gesture at any age.
But instead I up the ante.

"When I meet him—or her, or them—
you'll be the first to know." Grandma looks at me
as if she's come all the way to the theater,
only to find the lobby dark.

I try to explain what I feel about gender:
that I'd rather be a spirit already
than go on living in a fixed body.
I'm quick to say I'm not suicidal,

that I'm not trans or questioning—
worried she'll fill in the blanks
with the few words she knows. Instead, I say,
"I don't buy into your binaries."

I say, "You have to understand,
my generation looks at men's and women's restrooms
the way yours looked at segregated ones."
I can tell she doesn't want to argue, but she sighs.

"Isn't it enough that I love you, child?" she says.
I assure her it is, and I assure her it isn't.
"It's never going to be good enough, is it?"
And I ask her if it ever was.

LABELS

1

Do you remember
the first time
you heard the word

and it felt like
your name

and you wondered
who saw you wear it?

Did it sting
how they said it
with fear?

Or did their hatred
make it more
powerful?

How about later,
when you first heard
your word again

in a different light?
You wanted to hug the stranger

who gave grace
back to you.

Though it wasn't you,
not yet.
Not even to yourself.

2

Grandma would take me shopping.
First in her section, then in mine.
I'd touch the lace, the velvet,
and she'd smack my hands,
no matter how clean they were.

I'd help her pick out dresses,
happy to wait as she tried them on.
We had a system: thumbs-up
meant it fit right, flattering her;
a scrunched nose meant yes,
but no. Usually she'd decide
on her own, regardless. But I loved it
when I'd nod or smile and she'd beam,
as if my blessing were a true blessing,
sealing the deal.
                    And once,
I talked her into trying on a dress
so far from her own taste
that it seemed a personal victory.
And though she didn't buy it,
Grandma thanked me, telling me
I had good taste. "It's just not me,"
she said, admiring herself in the mirror.

But in the boys' section, it was different.
I didn't care what she picked out for me,
none of the clothes as colorful
or as intricate as I wanted them to be.

I suppose she thought I was tired
when I refused to try them on.
And so we rushed, and I disappeared
back inside my body,
eager to be home again.

"I'm lucky you don't care
about labels," she would say,

after passing some boy
having a fit
over a trendy shirt,
too much for his parents.

And I'd agree, happy
my grandma
thought
she was lucky.

SELFLESS

Dancing alone in my room,
I pretend I'm someone else.

It took so long to clear away my messes,
to move furniture, make some space.
Now that song that drew me in is gone.
Replaced by a strange new beat.

I move my hips, wishing I could summon joy.
Instead, I feel fake, a solid trying to be fluid.

I thought if I surrounded myself
with objects I love, I might love myself,
my body. Instead, I made it worse.

For days I've refused to touch myself, or look.
I closed my eyes in the shower
until I cut myself shaving.
There's always a mirror I could fall into,
a screen to remind me of my skin.
There's always some asshole
calling me the wrong thing.
Asking me questions so personal
I'm not equipped to answer them.

But there is also that precious time of day
when I'm not alone. When I have friends
flocking about me, as if I'm a widow
with a bag of bread.

Better to be Hunter's friend, I realize.
Seeing him at his party, happy with Vanilla,
I know there's a side to them I would never hear about.
And I don't want to be the fly in their honey.

THE GREAT AND POWERFUL OZ

Sometimes I look at a boy
    and he sees me looking
        and I watch as he takes it in
            the possibility I posit
                simply by being
                    visible
And sometimes that same boy
    hardens his back tightens his lips
        and looks away so deliberately
            it's like he wants me to see him
                not looking *not* seeing me
                    like he wants to make me
                      disappear
Sometimes though
    there's kerosene on the rag in the bucket
        and fumes fill the envelope of air
            for hours before some stranger comes
                with his half-finished cigarette
                careless

Sometimes walking in a room feels dangerous
    sometimes for me and sometimes them
        disgust or lust it hardly matters
            assuming a boy sees what I do
                in himself or in me
                and panics

I assume that's why I close off too
    why when someone looks I can disappear
        with or without them
            going cold

I close my eyes without closing them
I go to that place inside myself

I imagine there's a stage there
and a spotlight hot as my heart
one I might clomp up onto

becoming who they see
while still being who I am

SEX TALK

1

Sometimes, meeting a boy my age, a young man,
I can't decide what version of myself to be,
and hold off speaking until the last possible second.
I wait for him to ask me questions. And if he doesn't,
I'm mysterious and brooding, a delicate wafer
to be placed on the tongue until it's dissolved.
If he asks who I am, I tell him who I want to be;
if he asks who I want to be, I make jokes
about the limitless ambitions of my people—
a people I've invented, as if there are whole villages like me
hiding somewhere, in the woods along the interstate.
If he asks a more ordinary question, I answer it and wait
for his real question. Because there's always one more
waiting on the other side. What was your mother like, say,
or, Do you feel more or less yourself, dressed like that?

There's always something more to know. And if he asks,
I'll tell him almost everything, keeping nothing for myself.

2

Abercrombie likes being a guy's first.
He says it reminds him to be a person,
because he says most guys want that
their first time.
                    To me,
Ab sounds like a drug addict
when he talks about sex
as if it were merely a chemical.
                         Still,
he likes it when a guy is curious,
treating Ab like the exception to some innate rule.

It makes him feel, well, exceptional.
And I get that. I want that, too.
But I don't believe him
when Ab insists he can tell
when a straight guy's curious,
can tell closeted gay guys
from "out-of-towners,"
which is his name for them.
                              "Can't," he'll say.
"I've got a buddy over from out of town."
"Later, bro," I'll say back, dropping down
to my deepest voice.

Sometimes I wonder
if what Abercrombie actually wants
is immortality,

to be remembered as a god
with his glowing tan arms and body
hard as carved marble.

Because I know while he's taking a guy's virginity
he isn't really having sex—not for himself,
not how he prefers it—but is instead
giving them a fantasy they'll think about
for the rest of their lives, probably.

3

Sex is power. I believe that.
But it isn't all-powerful.

It's the dot at the end of a question mark, sure.
But also the cup of tea you let go cold.
It can be the most natural part of human nature
or what makes someone afraid to live at all.

It depends on how comfortable someone is
being a self, alone with the universe.

Which is what we are, always, even when surrounded
by the people who know us best.

4

My friends are part of me.
Sometimes I fear they're the bigger part.

5

When a guy asks what my first time was like,
I sometimes tell him it was perfect, describing how I was wooed
by a handsome gentleman. I might explain that he took me
to a rooftop terrace and fed me grapes right off the vine. I sometimes claim
I don't know what happened. I just found myself there
in a man's arms, my heart expanding
twenty times the size it needs to be. Or that it was love
that made me stay on that roof until dawn,
my new lover crooning at daybreak, and that this
has since become our love theme, the song that plays
in the film version of our meeting, still playing in my head.

Or else I might answer that it was good, not great.
Explaining that I'm still waiting for perfection—
a challenge, then, for the person I'm with.

But I never tell them the truth,
that I'm all talk.
More the imaginary ripe fruit on my invented terrace
than a fed mouth or a feeling hand.
More Vanilla than Hunter, and in fact
not ready. Still "pure," whatever that means.
Innocent, if you can call someone that
who knows better, who walks the line
in heels, knowing how he's seen.

NAMING ONESELF

"Okay, Princess," my grandma's husband would say—
mumble, really—
once I'd already gotten my way
and Grandma was cutting the rib meat from the bone,
so I could pretend it was never an animal.

Nightmares call me Candy. I have shit for brains.
And in the morning, on the bus, I hear it:
"Hey, Shitforbrains, that's my seat."
I get out of the bully's way,
dreaming of ways to fight him, pre-coffee.

I hear them call me Clown, and I turn
because it's someone I care about calling me.
But every time I half want to ask: Is it my painted smile?
My blush-red cheeks? The pink polyester hair
I'm trying out today? Or do I make you laugh?

Yet, inside me there's a curious vacuum,
which insists on being called something or other.
Princess, I think. For Grandpa. *Kiddo*, I think for Grandma.
Coolio, Ab sometimes calls me. But why? I don't get it.
When the name Clown started, I thought, *Sure,*

let Hunter name me, the way a parent names a child
without it fitting yet. I could let love allow it,
could take on his word
and reshape it in my mind until it fit.
But not that word. Not now. Not knowing what I know
about my own swan heart.

Yet how do I take the word away
without replacing it? And how do I make the swap
without everyone needing to know
how I define myself?

I want something ancient. Something timeless.
I wonder if there's a myth I don't yet know
in which someone like me
can't be pinned down. Not being Greek,
I stop myself from searching.
Besides, my name's already in me.
I can feel it, reaching back at me
as I wonder. The way a fountain
reaches up and down at once.

Star? I ask myself. Why not?
But I'm not a star, not yet.
I'm a promise to the universe,
a mountain still being born
or whatever a wind is called in space—
made not of air, but magnetism.
An angel on the way.

Angel? I think. And, thinking it, I smile.
Remembering the wings of my new heart.
Not male or female, masculine or feminine,
but landing beautifully in the mind.
Muscular, from having flown.
Graceful, born of spirit.

I go to the mirror to try it on.
Once I look, I realize:
An angel has already arrived.

HOW AM I DIFFERENT?

Sometimes, in a poem, there's a moment
when a little girl is running,
and the poet doesn't say if she's on the street
or in the woods or what,
only that she's afraid.
And already, I feel for her, afraid,
running as fast as a little girl can.
Which is crazy fast, and still
something's gaining on her.

And sometimes, in a poem, there's a moment
when time doesn't feel right,
and the girl, running, mistakes her own footsteps
for those of a stranger chasing her.
I feel her panic
as if I know her
and know myself through her.
Does that make sense?

And sometimes, writing poems, it works,
and sometimes it doesn't.
Sometimes everything a person sees or senses
gets probed for meaning
as if the poet believes only in logic.
Instead of reading the girl's face,
so the real reader can,
the poet's busy reading the marsh light
reflected in her tears.
And still I feel I know her,
even though I can't. Even though
the poet hasn't told me enough.

I've held the truth
back from myself.

And sometimes, most times,
the poet sits down to write a poem about one thing
and ends up telling something else.
Something truer. So what
if he never ends up telling you
the girl's okay, she's fine, it's all made up,
and instead turns you around
to face him. And he says something
he's never told anyone, not even Vanilla.

That it hurts to know and love someone
all the way.
That it hurts every time they deny you
knowing more.
Not the same hurt, over and over
but different pain
each time
always new, always
deepening

as if it's wrong to ask
in the first place.
As if it's wrong to want more.
And somehow worse
than not getting what I want
is the feeling that I'm wrong
for feeling like this.
Like maybe I feel too much
and should calm down.

Normal people aren't like this.
Normal, sane people don't go on loving
someone who keeps stopping them
from loving them fully.
Normal people don't read poems
about girls running
and think of Vanilla
running away from nothing
and punch the wall in the library.

Normal people don't read poems
and think, Why is he doing this to me?
Why am I letting him
break my heart
right in front of me
with all these witnesses?

And then I remember that normal people
don't matter much. Not to me.
Because they don't know Vanilla like I do.
Normal people don't
see him smiling and think,
I want to make him smile like that
all over his body.

Normal people don't
care about anybody but themselves,
and they certainly don't
care about me, and they
certainly don't read poems.

CONDITIONAL

Hunter doesn't want to go to the dance, suddenly.
But Red says we have to. She's on the committee.

"Don't make me go by myself," I beg him.
But he says he's not in the mood to "perform" for her. Or me.

As if he'd be acting, lying, if we held hands, leaned in.
"I haven't been entirely honest with you," he says.

"It's eating me alive inside."
My heart sinks. I knew it, somehow.

Hunter still hasn't said what he means,
and I don't yet know how bad it is. But my heart seems to.

"What?" I say, not sure which misery I'd choose, if I could.
"You're scaring me."

"I've just been talking," he says. "To guys, I mean. Online.
But before you say anything, I need you to know

I always say I have a boyfriend. And I haven't lied to you
or cheated, really. I mean, I'm telling you now."

This is how I know I must still love him:
because it hurts so bad, hearing it.

And the fact that it's my choice if it's a fight or not,
that it's my call if we explode, like I want to. Right now,

that part seems as cruel as the rest of it.
But what else did I expect?

The first to come out, Hunter pushed me out.
The first to hit puberty, he begged for sex.

And when I finally felt ready to give in a little,
he barreled forward, single-minded as a bull charging,

and knocked the wind right out of me.

HIDE-AND-SEEK

I can't find Vanilla. I've looked everywhere.
So I ask his best friend if he's okay.

Red looks up at me like I'm crazy,
not bothering to swallow her bite of bologna.

"If you, of all people, aren't sure,
then I think you have your answer, Sweetie."

TO BE OR NOT TO BE?

1

Every choice I make, lately, seems as if I'm choosing him or me.
Or like I'm choosing myself or some other self
that isn't me, but could be, if only I chose it.

All fall it's been like this. Now it's winter, and I'm lonely.
Some of it is the cold, the dying leaves.
But most of it isn't.

I go to the places we used to go, when we were starting out,
hoping to feel something, to know if it's all in my head.
But everything has changed, inside and out.

The playground where we used to kiss
has no slide now. The fairgrounds are an empty field.
Even our honeysuckle patch is gone. Turned into a paved lot

behind the middle school. An annex for faculty parking.
I text Hunter in tears when I realize. And he takes too long
to text back. *Things change,* he says, as if it were that simple.

It's up to us to keep them alive, he goes on, *as memories.*
And sure, part of it is that I'm not ready for change.
But mostly it's not the change I fear, but the loss.

The parts that I don't choose to give up
slipping away, too, out of my control.
You don't even care, I write back. *It's not a metaphor.*

But it makes him angry.
You're the one who didn't even notice until now.
And what can I say? He's right.

He must have noticed, months ago or longer,
slipped the sad fact silently into his heart,
so I never knew it.

And I don't know if I should be upset.
On one hand, he's protecting me. On the other,
I want some choice in the matter.

Which is to say, I don't know if I should be upset,
but I am.

2

The next time we hang out, Hunter takes me to the park.
He says he has to now
or he'll regret it forever.

There's snow and ice,
and the park looks dead
as any frozen thing.

"I'm cold," I warn him.
But we're almost there,
and I'm not as cold as I'm pretending.

Hunter shows me a patch of brambles, heavy with ice.
He points toward the wall behind them,
asks me to look at something there.

I refuse to weave through the vines in my new coat,
refuse to follow him any farther.
Not into those brambles, not home, nowhere.

In fact, I should go now.
"I should go," I say.
But Hunter won't let me.

He blocks me with his body,
as he never has before. Forceful. Insistent.

And I can't help but play the betrayal card

as I pound against his chest, sobbing.
"I shouldn't have brought you," he says.
"Now you'll hate this, too."

But I don't understand what he means.

Where are we?

TO BE OR NOT TO BE?

Clown asks if it isn't a little mean
for me to stay together with Vanilla
even if my heart isn't in it.

And I ask, which is worse,
to dump him or to wait for him
to realize it's already over?

"Depends what you're asking,"
Clowns says, looking serious for once.
"Which is worse for him

or which is worse for you?"

LOVE STORY

The night of the dance, Hunter tells me a story.
He tells it to me against my will, on the walk to my house,
while I try to ignore Red's increasingly urgent texts.
And it's not far into Hunter's story
when I realize it's a story about us.
He tells me his side of meeting me, his version
of our kiss on the Ferris wheel
and on the boardwalk, under fireworks.
He remembers things I don't. Going on and on
about how long a wait it was for a hot dog.
And as I remember it for myself, I realize
he must have hid his impatience well.
Because all my memories are of him smiling at me.
Not even watching the fireworks. Watching me instead.
Then Hunter's telling me about the night we came out.
In horrific, tedious detail.
How we timed it elaborately, knowing our parents
would insist on talking to one another.
We knew my mom and dad would try to keep us
from going to the dance that night,
and we knew we could count on his mom
to defend us, repeating that we hadn't done anything wrong.
"Excuse me, Nina, for interrupting," my mom said,
"but I think we should discuss this as adults.
Without the kids on the line."
"They're hardly kids," Hunter's mother had said.
They fought. I cried.
But Hunter remembers it differently.
In his version, the conversation ends right there
and we're off to the dance! To come out, all over again—
only to our friends and school and world.
We're late, and everyone's been waiting for us.
"But we look dashing in our matching tuxedoes,"
Hunter says. "Classic black and white."
"Nice touch," I say, forgetting that I'm angry at him.

I grin at the thought of our eighth-grade selves in formal wear,
then sigh the smile out until I'm empty again.
If Hunter notices, he ignores it,
painting a pretty picture of the evening, half-truth,
half-fantasy, until I don't know what is what.
In Hunter's version, it's as if the middle school dance
had been a pride parade. Bunting and confetti
in every color of the rainbow. The smell of popcorn
filling the gymnasium. But he remembers correctly
what music was playing when he asked me to dance
the first time. Along with what song was playing later,
when he asked again. When I finally agreed,
we stepped out in front of everybody,
two boys taking to the floor.

"Just don't let go of my hand," Hunter whispers to me now,
just like he did that night.
"Whatever you do, don't let go."
We're walking. And I'm cold. And my eyes are watery,
but not from crying this time.
When Hunter slides his fingers against mine, it feels so good.
Still I close my eyes as I walk, blocking out everything
but the memory of the song he's named.
I play it in my head, pretending we're still at that dance.
I build the scene for myself, detail by detail,
wanting it to be real, only
it isn't.
"What happens next?" I ask him,
not wanting either of us to be sad anymore.
"You can tell it if you want," Hunter says, but I don't want to.
I want him to tell his side of everything,
up through to when he tells me why I'm not enough.
I want him to hear our story come out his own throat
so that he can either hear how ridiculous he sounds
or tell me what he's really thinking.
What other parts of the story I don't yet know.
"No," I say, "you," my voice trembling.
"Well, naturally," he says, still holding my hand,
"all of our classmates erupted in oohs and aahs.

Followed by applause. Followed by the deejay
cutting immediately to the latest ultragay megamix.
I mean, what else would happen
if two middle school senior boys—in tuxes, let's not forget—
slow-danced in front of hundreds
of their not-entirely-self-aware peers?"

I say, "All I remember is Mandi Larson saying 'Ew'
and a few kids shushing her. And then
after the song, there were a million questions.
And then everyone was talking about us."
I wipe my nose, letting go of his hand.
"No, no," Hunter says, grabbing it again,
not even caring that it's wet and gross.
"Whatever you do," he repeats, sounding serious,
"don't. Let. Go."
We both smile. But it's the kind that hurts
because there's pain and confusion underneath.
"I shouldn't have brought you to the park before," Hunter says.
"I've been looking forward to it for so long,
and now I ruined it." I want to tell Hunter he hasn't ruined anything,
but I don't know if that's true.
"I mean it's winter," he says. "It all died back.
You couldn't even see it."
"See what?" I ask him,
and he looks at me, confused, then refuses to say.
Headlights appear in the distance, and my instinct
is to let go of his hand. I'm not sure why, exactly.
It's not like we live in the kind of town
where two boys can't hold hands. And yet
I don't want whoever's in the car
to see us and think anything. To see how old we are
and think because we're holding hands
they know everything.
"Whatever you do," Hunter starts to say,
because he knows me. He can feel my grip
loosening as the car approaches. "Don't," he warns me.
So it hurts us equally when I do.

TRIAL & ERROR

You'll blame sex. But it isn't the sex I can't live without.
Sure, I want it. I want to crawl off and drink in the dark.
To feel the talk of our skin, finally. Then thrum beside you.
I want to really know: bliss, taken in ever-replenishing sips.

And to sleep in secret, then wake again, our bodies still touching.
I want to plead like that, having everything,
wanting nothing. If I could only have you, I thought,
the rest of my life could stop mattering so much.

I wanted to keep a secret and tell it, too. I wanted to know you,
that's all. Know more, know better.
I wanted to learn what you like through trial and error.
Mastering your pleasure, as if it were art.

And that, too, was greedy—but as all love is.
I wanted a key to a city, to be offered endless entrance—
but less to come knocking than to feel so welcome.
I wanted to be as much at home in your skin as mine,

to feel complete within ourselves. As fully as my mind and heart
had already claimed us to be.

> You'll blame sex. But you shouldn't.
> You'd be wrong.

I only said I wanted it because I thought I knew the answer.
What hurt most was having been proven so wrong. I thought,
How else am I mistaken? What else might you one day refuse?
It's doubt, not sex, that did it. Turning every answer into a new
   question.

SECRETS

1

We've never had secrets. Not until now.
Hunter has a safe in his room—a gift
from his dad before he left—and though
even his mom doesn't know the combination,
I do. Along with all its contents:
Polaroid pictures of The Gang, condoms "just in case,"
pills he's holding for Abercrombie.

There are innocent things, too,
barely worth mentioning:
cash and cards and collectibles.
Love notes. His and mine, both.
All of it made somehow more valuable
by secrecy, proximity to danger.

Hunter has an email account
no one else knows about,
and he gave me the password.
He uses it for porn site log-ins,
and to sign up for newsletters
he doesn't intend to read.
He sends himself his favorite photos of me,
gifting them to the cloud like backward rain.
I felt like something innocent
made dangerous
simply by being there, in his hoard,
among all those men.
No one writes him there
but spammers and creeps,
and occasionally me.

If he's logged out of his real account,
I know what he's probably doing.

Careful! You'll go blind! I wrote to him once,
wanting him to think of me, during.
But he didn't think it was funny.
And when he didn't write back, I wrote,
Save some love for me.
Which wasn't funny, either.

"It's all for you, if you want it, you know,"
he said the next day, in a weirdly good mood.
"Save me, Vanilla! I don't want to go blind!"
He picked me up and put me down.
He looked me over, head to toe,
as if I were his number one reason
to want to see the world.

2

That was before. Right when it started.
Lately he's never in a good mood.
When I tease him, it hurts him.
He doesn't blush, but steam.

3

Hunter's started working out.
He has actual muscles. The kind
we used to make fun of.
He's no Abercrombie, but it's the same.
And even that I can understand, if I try to.
Times change. People do.
That's what I'm told, over and over.

At some point he changed our password.

4

When Hunter catches me reading his poetry journal,
it turns into the biggest fight we've ever had.

"Not all of me is yours!" he screams.
"I didn't think any of you was," I say.
"I wish that was true," he tells me,
like it hurts to be loved this much.
And when we finally calm down,
I try to make light of it.
        "That must be quite a poem," I say,
            "if you're not begging me to read it."
And then we're fighting all over again.

5

I don't know what it is about our fights lately
that makes them dark inside.
Impossible to navigate.
Once blood is boiling, it boils over.

And that black hole
sucks everything in
until Hunter seems to want me
to be as angry as he is.
Or maybe he wants to see how close we can get
before we cease to exist.

6

"I forgive you," I say,
trying to fix it.
"I'm not asking for forgiveness,"
Hunter replies. And somehow it's worse
having to wonder if he's even sorry.

"I'm not saying I don't love you anymore," Hunter says.
"Only that I can't keep loving you like I have."

We've never had a fight like this.
Usually when it's over, we're stronger after.
We know each other better, not worse.

Usually after a fight, we kiss, we hug,
and it feels like we're sorry
we fought in the first place.

But this time, it's different.
Nothing I say can fix it.
I don't even understand what's broken.
It's like he *wants* to be angry.
Needs to hate me right now.

But why?

7

On my way home,
to my own house after school,
I text with Red.

I don't know what I did.

And at first she doesn't answer,
even though I can see she's read it.

I need you. I'm sorry! Please!

You know what you did,
she says. Like it's our friendship I mean.

But Red's so smart, she figures it out.
She asks why I care what she thinks,

and I tell her it's because she knows me
better than anyone, I think.
Maybe even Hunter.

She asks if it's possible I didn't do anything.
I know she doesn't mean sex,
but my heart latches onto it.

He looked at me like I make him sick.

Red asks what she can do, but there's nothing.
There's nothing anyone can.

Except maybe me.

FIRST-PERSON ACCOUNT

I didn't want there to be ceremony.
But I didn't want it be ordinary, either.
And when I pictured it, it never felt right.
I'd imagine telling Vanilla it was over,
and it still wasn't. No matter how many times
I went through it in my head, trying on the feeling.

So when I finally did it, as gently as I could,
I confess I felt relief.

"I think we both know things haven't been good," I said.
"And neither of us is happy. We haven't been
for a long time now." And Vanilla agreed to every reason,
as if each were self-evident. And I thought,
Whoa, this is going so well. He agrees!

Then the waiter came by, and Vanilla actually smiled.
And that's when I knew he still didn't get it.

"I'm sorry," I said. "I can't be boyfriends anymore."
I watched his face for recognition, expecting
the pieces to fall in place. Maybe he would sigh
or maybe he would explode. There was no telling.
But then his eyes started to fill.

And I thought, *Whatever I've done, I've done it.*
Panic fizzed in my brain, an urgent dread.
But I knew it was the right thing to do.
And so I felt a strange pride I tried to hide from him.
I guess I couldn't hide it, though. Right in front of me
the guy I loved, who loved me back for so long,
hardened into a stranger, right before my eyes.

THE LAST KISS IS THE CRUELEST

I don't want anyone anymore
to sing me to sleep, to guess my wishes,
to kiss my ring finger.

It's hard enough
being a person.
Why be two,
like I was with you,
feeling for us both?

I don't want you to be sorry, Hunter,
to be sad for me, to tell everyone
you did it the kindest way you could.
Then watch me from a distance
like a cowardly dragon
who bites the knight with poison,
then slinks off to watch him die
from the safety of its dark cave.

There is no kind way, Hunter,
to take it all back, to tell someone
you might not have meant it
all along. The longing
general,
the feeling
chemical, not special.

You don't get to be the hero here, Hunter.
Not now or ever again.

I don't want it to be you
to remind me how it was,
to assure me how it can be
again someday, maybe,
if you feel like it.

I don't want it to be you
to thread the fogged future
with silver linings,
or to shine a light,
as if we might see through this.

I don't want it to be you
to reach for my tears,
thinking, *I've got this.*

You don't got this, Hunter.
Any of it.

I don't want it to be you anymore.

UNTIED BALLOON

How can you do that to a person,
fill them so up with love that they're full.
And then let them go?

and like that, it isn't poetry anymore. I don't want it to be a poem because if it isn't, it won't be me. Sad little poet, leaving his soul behind for a night.

I have Abercrombie with me. He's dating the door guy, who lets us in. But twenty minutes later, Ab's gone. Like it was the plan all along. I check the bathroom and both bars. Coat check. The back patio. But there's no sign of him. I'm blissfully alone.

I say blissfully because I don't know the right word. Not this time. If Clown were with me, he'd know. But he isn't. Not even Clown can know about this. I want to dive forward, out of my life and into the next. I want to be claimed, made real, more adult, stripped of any innocence left. And I think this will do it, finally. Finding someone like me, or someone nothing like me, either one. I want someone to pull me by the hand through the lights to kiss me in a dark corner.

I thought I'd be scared. Not of being seen, but of being known. For someone from reality to see me and judge me, knowing what I want. But I'm searching every set of eyes, and I don't recognize a single person here. And now all those eyes I was looking into are searching back. My body, my mouth. Plumbing my own eyes for confirmation. Who will it be among them? I let every one of them stare and savor. Even a guy I'm not into, leering at me from a shadowy couch in the corner. I flex at the thought of him waving me over. Seconds later, he's waving me over. Magic.

I shake my head, but I'm smiling. My blush his consolation prize.

But it isn't enough. He's standing up. Coming over to me. He's pock-marked, sad-looking, but he straightens his spine, looking hungry as I am. So I stop smiling, shake my head with pity on my face. He walks right by me, as if I've read him wrong. As if it was never me he was looking at. Yeah, right.

The whole thing makes me sad suddenly. Like, why does it have to be like this?

I pour myself some water from a pitcher on the bar. My hand shakes as I lift the cup to my lips. I'm looking around, and it's like no one sees me. The eyes now seem ice cold. As if by turning that one guy down, I've turned them all down and no one likes me now. As if I think I'm better than them 'cause I'm younger. But I don't. I feel the opposite.

The song changes, and it's suddenly too loud to think. I head for the bathroom, telling myself Ab must be here somewhere. But turning the corner, I run straight into a guy who is dashing for the dance floor. My water and his beer both splash at our feet. His flimsy cup cracks in his hand while mine hits the ground. It isn't glass, so it doesn't shatter. Instead, the hard plastic bounces with a spray of ice clattering. Which is somehow worse.

I curse as I bend to pick it up, nearly tripping the guy again as I scoop the dirty ice up, best I can. The guy's cursing, too, now, but not at me. At the cup, leaking beer down his wrist and arm. And I watch as he sets it down on the bar behind me. Blots his inner elbow with a pinch of small white napkins.

If this is his favorite song, he's missing it.

But he asks if I'm okay. And as I look at him in the face, finally, I catch a smile.

I tell him yeah and sorry; he says the same.

"My bad," he tells me. "Should have watched where I was going."

Then he asks what I was drinking so he can replace it.

"It's no big deal," I tell him, not wanting to admit I was drinking water.

"Let me buy you a drink," he says, like he really wants to.

"Okay," I reply. I wish I could figure out his age. But it's dark. He has a real deep voice. And he's handsome, I know that. He seems kind enough. I tell myself that right now his kindness is all that matters.

I notice someone waving to him from the dance floor. But Drink Guy ignores him, leaning across the bar. I stare at the whole back of him as it stretches and relaxes again. He glances at the bartender, then me, then back, then me again. As if he's afraid he'll lose me if he stares off too long. Or afraid we'll never be served if he dives into my gaze for too long. Once he's ordered, his every attention is on me.

He asks if I'm going to the college nearby. Turns out he's a freshman there, and moved to the area this fall.

"None of my friends are gay," he says. "It sucks."

I tell him that all of my friends are gay, which can suck, too. And though it's an exaggeration, it feels honest.

And then things stop making sense. We go to the patio, to drink in relative quiet. Talking about the song I made him miss. And it's nice, but not nice enough. He's sexy as hell, but not sexy enough suddenly to keep me distracted. Maybe it's because I'm no longer alone. Maybe it's because I have half a drink in me and am feeling the gravity of the night. But I'm thinking of Vanilla suddenly, at every turn. The two of us in college someday or going out together on our twenty-first birthday. For so long recently, I forced myself to focus on the negative—because otherwise I would have been trapped forever in that horrible feeling. But now that I'm free, and right here on the brink of whatever it is I'm doing, I'm picturing Vanilla here at the table with College Boy and me. And the imagined presence feels so sweet, it destroys me.

"Well, nice meeting you," he says. And I realize I should apologize all over. But he asks if he can text me, and I say sure. We exchange numbers and first names.

The whole thing feels so normal. Like friends. And I think, *No no no.* I can't stand another friend. It's a lover I want. So I ask if he really has to go. And when he says he does, I ask if I can go with him.

"You're trouble," he says. "I like it."

But he has a test in the morning. And a roommate.

"Besides," he says, "I like you enough not to mess this up."

College Boy says he's a "long game" guy. Says I seem like I am, too.

I tell him with a groan, "You have no idea."

EMPATHY (WHAT NOT TO SAY)

I thought the truth would be my savior.
And maybe it is, if Vanilla is what I needed saving from.

Reader,
do me a favor.

If you ever make the same mistake,
and break someone's heart,

don't try to heal it immediately
by reminding him of all your favorite memories.

If his heart is broken, he can't feel
what you need him to, not yet.

Instead you'll be training him to hate
those same moments. It won't only be the photos he burns,

the figurines he smashes, the emails he deletes.
It will be as if you never did or felt those things together,

having lost some of the good
in that same fire

never again able to bring those moments up
without his heart clenching a little, to check.

I NEVER MEANT TO HAUNT YOU

I think of our love now
as one might an object
so far removed from use
but still useful in the mind:
an hourglass, an abacus,
a broken pocket watch—
hell, any watch, working
or not—all of them earnest
and useful and beautiful,
despite having been
sidestepped by the current.
Each of them worth keeping
around in the hoard, if only
for the meat of metaphor.

Except, my dear—
no longer mine—
you aren't around
any more than you are
broken. I see you
as one sees a ghost,
out of the side of his eye;
when I try to look,
you're gone. Evading
my every tenderness
the way a spirit
avoids acknowledgment,
or the way a bird escapes
a feeding hand—
the way I dodge, too,
turning off
down an empty hall,
hoping not to see you.

But please, Vanilla,
never worry
that I want you out of my life
any more now than I ever did.

If I am a ghost, it's all mercy.
It isn't you I circumvent,
taking the long way around.
It's the look in your eye
I almost catch. The trembling
I'm never close enough
to see for sure, but which
I feel, nonetheless.
If I could only save you
from your doublethink,
I would kindly vanish.

No one wants to be the weapon
lodged in the heart, to be
healed around
so that the wound
retains his shape,
even after he's gone.
I'd much prefer to be
a memory, even if bittersweet,
than the present cause
you casually resent.

What terrifies me most
is the thought that your pain
might cause you to forget,
the way trauma wipes the mind
clean with its hatchet,
and that all of the good
will be severed with the bad,
so that someday
you'll finally
look at me again,
but you'll want to flee

without knowing why,
having forgotten me.

SUMMER ANNIVERSARY

In the same way that I can remember the beach
once it's winter and the sun no longer burns,
I can think of our first date now—the one that counts
because we knew what it was. (What we were.)
His big brother drove us to a restaurant
in walking distance to a movie theater.
He dropped us off, a big smile on his face.
Chris had known me for years already,
but it was still a little awkward, waving goodbye,
as if he knew something we didn't.
As soon as we were alone, Hunter told me
the whole ride over Chris had doled out advice.
"Don't treat him like a friend anymore," he said,
"or you'll stay friends forever." He warned him not to wait
to see if I wanted a good-night kiss,
claiming, "It's harder to tell than you'd think."
And, "Don't wait for him to lean in first. Just go for it."
Hunter told me all of this before the appetizer came.
"I guess I'm already breaking his rules," he said,
and I told him it was okay if we were friends forever.
"Does he know we've already kissed?" I asked.
"Yeah," he said. "He says it will be different . . .
but I'll stop talking about him now.
And I'll also stop telling you everything that crosses my mind,
the moment it crosses my mind. Starting now."
And then he told me I looked nice. "Real nice, actually."
"Okay," he said, with finality in his voice. "Starting now."
"Did your brother tell you to say that?" I asked,
but Hunter insisted he came up with it all on his own.
"I don't mind if you tell me what you're thinking," I told him.
"Good," he said, "because I like telling you.
And I don't think I could keep anything from you."
After dinner, we crossed the mall parking lot as the lamps came on.
"I'm going to kiss you now," Hunter said. "Why wait?"
We both leaned in

190

and Chris was right, it did feel different.

Because it wasn't the least bit funny. In fact,

it seemed intensely serious, even though we had just been laughing.

I closed my eyes, letting myself settle into the new.

I could do this forever, I thought. And then I peeked

and caught him peeking, too. "I kind of wish

we weren't going to the movie now," he said.

"Sorry, I'm doing it again, aren't I?"

"'Starting now,'" I said. "'Starting now.'"

And that became the night's joke, which in turn became

an inside joke. And after the movie, after our real good-night kiss,

after Chris texted asking if we were ready.

After Hunter replied: *No! Never! Leave us here!*

And after Hunter walked me to my door like a gentleman, I said,

"I know you want a kiss, but my parents are probably watching."

And he said, "I didn't say it that time, did I?"

I told him he didn't need to 'cause I could read his mind.

"Oh yeah?" he said. "What am I thinking *now?*"

"You're right," I joked. "It was the perfect first date."

"Close," he said. And then I couldn't stop smiling.

UNEQUAL AFFECTION

For our first anniversary, Hunter gave me his favorite shirt,
the one I borrowed for photo day and threatened
never, ever to return. He wrapped it and everything.
Even replaced the one missing button to match.

I love you more than my favorite _____,
the card had said.

At first I didn't get it.
I opened the box and parted the tissue paper.
"Shirt!" I squealed.
It wasn't just *like* the shirt. It *was* the shirt.
And he loved me more, he said so.
He made it mine, like he was.

"Fill in the blank,"
he said, kissing me.
"It could be anything. Name it.
I promise I love you more."

All day we played that game, kissing.
"More than your favorite movie?" I'd ask.
"Yes. I do. I love you more than *The Lion King.*"
He loved me more than yellow, more than bacon chocolate.
More than "Hey Ya!," toucans, and John Lennon combined.
More than his favorite cereal, and much, much more
than the month of May.

Then I thought I had him stumped. I asked,
"More than your favorite holiday?"
Hunter paused much longer than he had before.
"It's okay," I said, a little glad there was something
for us to aspire to. "Wait, wait," Hunter said. "Not so fast!"
He reached across the table to take my hand.
"I do. I do love you more."

Our server came with our check, which I snatched up.

"Well, this is my present," I said. And he thanked me.

I smiled and paid, and then we left.

"What *is* your favorite holiday?" I asked in the parking lot.

Hunter rolled his eyes. "Our anniversary, duh."

BACKING AWAY

If the story were told in reverse,
our last kiss, which was actually our first,
would seem the happiest.

Tears wouldn't be something lost but gained,
and instead of pulling away needlessly, nervous,
we would know only how to reach suddenly for each other.

Each caress would slow, with uncertain parting,
as if inches from each other our creeping hands
deciphered their own affectionate regrets.

Your early exit from the room
would begin with a welcoming embrace
before you slowly back out through the door,

smiling with recognition.
The emptiness after would be the same
as the emptiness before,

only gentler. Like hearing the same story twice.
You can tell it however you like, Hunter.
But from now on, this is how I choose to recall our love.

A series of mistakes undone, rumors unheard.
The strange fights caused by prolonged silences.
How silly we look, answering our phones with a slam!

And now how happy we've become,
after all this time.
having only just met.

FIRST DATE

My first real date with College Boy,
we looked straight at the sun. Seriously.
He brought me to the campus observatory,
where a telescope, big as a sofa,
was pointed up through high windows.
He asked me if I trusted him,
and I said yes. Hoping
he wasn't trying to blind me.

I looked through the eyepiece,
and there it was, the sun's surface,
filtered red so I could see. And on it
were sunspots, like freckles on skin,
and bright flares that reminded me
of campfires or forest fires. The whole thing
looked like a storm. A wildfire pulled in
by its own gravity. Which is how I felt.
Wondering, while I looked at it,
was he looking at me? My smaller body.
My younger skin. Thin and relatively
hairless arms.

He smelled like a man, not a boy.
And I breathed in deep, amazed
I could smell him as he leaned close beside me.
I thought of the advice my brother had given me
before my first date with Vanilla.
I couldn't stop wondering what it would be like
to kiss this guy who was nothing like
the only boy I'd ever really kissed.

He was taller than me, broader than me.
And so I imagined standing on my toes
to kiss him, the way Vanilla had stood
to kiss me, pushing upward

so that our bodies aligned.
His tan biceps stretched the sleeves
of his polo shirt. I imagined
holding on to one with both hands
as he flexed and kissed me. When
would it happen? I pulled my eye away
from the plastic, and there he was.
His mouth. His thick lips.
The stubble on his chin I couldn't stop
staring at. For a week, since we met,
I'd been stalking his profiles.
I'd jerked off thinking
of what it would feel like
if his stubbly skin grazed my thigh.
Seeing it up close again,
I only wanted it more.

"What?" he said when he saw me looking,
his voice deeper than mine. "Nothing," I said,
but I knew nothing wouldn't cut it.
"The sun's pretty cool," I added,
and he either laughed or coughed.

"Want to get out of here?" he asked,
like I'd passed his test. And I said yes,
though he hadn't yet passed mine.
"I'd take you to my dorm,
but my roommate's there." Already
I was playing it out in my head,
what we could do if the roommate wasn't.

He started the engine, put his big hand
on my knee, asking,
"Where do you want to go?"
I gave him, "Anywhere." And this time
I knew it was a laugh. "Okay, bud."
He gave my knee a squeeze.

Was it true? Would I be willing to go
anywhere he chose? I realized I didn't

need to be. I just needed to be willing
to go wherever he actually took me.

We ended up at a marina,
where we sat at the end of a shaded dock.
There were people around us,
getting in and out of the water.
But I also felt alone with him,
his arm heavy on my shoulders,
and yet weightless. I leaned my head
to rest it on the curve below his neck.
I kept thinking, *How can I get closer still?*
even as we were pressed together.
My mind reeled, wanting all of him.

But I kept thinking about Vanilla, too.
What he would think if he saw or heard.
I knew he would think College Boy was handsome.
But would he think I was running away,
that I'd chosen his opposite?
I knew I had. I needed to.

"You alright?" College Boy boomed. And I nodded,
half lying again, half lying about everything.
Where I would go and what I'd been thinking.
About trusting him, when I knew I didn't.
But wasn't that exactly what I wanted?
Some guy who'd selfishly take from me
everything I no longer wanted?

The sound of the wind on the water.
The water on the wood.
The boats and the noise
of preparation. All the while
the sun beating down on the ripples, the waves.
The bright right cheek of the Earth
as we sat in our shade,
not saying anything. Feeling each other's
touch for the first time.

MANIFEST DESTINY

> *eventually everyone can hope for a turn at being wanted*
> —Thom Gunn

I have to hide my eagerness, swallow it down
with all of my saliva until my mouth is dry.

All eyes or none. All breath or none.
I'm not thinking of arousal, or anything.

I don't mean to play an instrument,
tune his hairs to chords,

but I put my hand to the skin at his ankle.
It could be any touch. My hand

could be any part of me. His ankle any part of him.
The way the wave swells, wholly.

It is the same as any beginning.
A tentative mark in his tangle of senses.

I don't want to hurry, for once. I want to slow down
and feel, my fingers

an awareness without form. I help him find
his knee again. His thigh, out then in, a continent.

Each separate hair
joining a swarm of pleasure

as my new king
relearns the bounds of his kingdom.

TIMID CORRESPONDENCE

Hey, Clown. Or is it really Angel now?
Regardless, yeah, I got your letter.
Thanks for saying you're sorry
for what happened to me.
And for not putting the blame on anyone.
Smart.

And thanks for what you said about honesty
and how you first believed in love because of me.
It made me feel a little less
like you had a part in it. (I sure hope not.)

Over time, it's started to feel like it was worth it.
And I can sigh, finally, and admit to myself
that someday I might "love again" . . .
I know what you mean about being embarrassed,
and, yeah, I know I'm welcome with The Gang.
Thanks. Really.

I'm glad I don't have to pretend to be happy with you.
It means a lot that you'd offer.
But I think I have to do this on my own.
I'm not ready to talk about why.

Do you know that play we saw
in seventh grade, where the rooster was an acrobat?
And the whole ending, he hopped around, doing flips,
suspended by bungee cords?
Well, I don't know if you remember, but
we sat next to each other.
It's kind of my first memory of you.
Anyway.
After the play ended, the whole audience
seemed to turn to one another, at once.
Eyes wide open, in the silence before the applause.

We all wanted to see each other's reactions,
but didn't want to say anything.
We weren't ready to word it precisely.
and didn't want to get it wrong.

That's what it feels like now.
For weeks I've been waiting for someone
to do more than stare at me.
Red has, but it's different with her.
Because we talked about it all as it happened.
And you know, she's a girl. It's different.

I don't want to disappear
but I'm not ready to be seen.
I need somebody to tell me I'm not crazy,
that I didn't drive him away,
that instead a fissure opened in the ground between us,
and suddenly we weren't close. And maybe
one of us could have jumped, but we didn't.

It matters to me what you think,
not only because you're his friend but
because you pay attention.
That made you scary as hell
when I thought you were my enemy.
But I don't now.
Even if you didn't say he made a mistake,
even if you didn't call him a total asshole,
you managed to make me feel a little less alone.
Which at this point feels like a big deal.
You're a big deal to me, Angel.
I'll see you around.

LIFE CYCLE

for Vanilla and Hunter (but for Vanilla more)

I watched it happen.
Slow as seasons changing.
Slow and unsteady
as learning to play an instrument
or watching a building go up.
Only it was coming down.

Not piece by piece, in an order
I could figure. But haphazardly,
as if only the doors inside were gone
and then the windows.
Then the whole south wall.

We could all see inside;
none of it was working anymore.

KEEPSAKE

What can be done with a card after it's read?
Or a pressed flower that smells like dust?
Nothing. Throw it away, right?

But I want to make something of it.
The way together we made a game
out of waiting.

I want an altar still, somewhere in my life,
where I can put him for safekeeping.
Or if not him, our innocence. Mine.

A single place in the center of the universe
where time doesn't exist
and one wish doesn't follow the other, but leads,

and whatever mistakes I make between now and later
don't count anymore, not the same as they did
when I had a promise to keep.

KEEPSAKE

Watching you toss it all,
I love and fear you all the more.

Love, knowing what's left is mine.
Fear—that's just empathy

for him and you and both of you.

I wondered what it would be like after.
But nothing else looks like this blankness.

How neither of you talk the same
or act the same, or are the same.

Like a wound in the ground we made.

And how the grass didn't grow back right.

GAY CARD

Hunter made me one. Even found a way to have it laminated.
We'd just come out to each other, were still only friends.
I tell myself it's a gay thing, not a Hunter thing, and that's why
    I've kept it.

Sometimes I wonder
if I was ever good to Hunter
the way he was to me, even as friends.

When I'm kind to myself, I think definitely yes.
Sometimes I'm not kind to myself, though,
and it's different.

I picture his shrine as it was when I last saw it,
wondering if it looked like trash or treasure.

Still other times, I'm hard on Hunter.
Then it's way worse. As if all those lovely things he did,
he didn't do for me, only for himself.
Tipping the scales every which way he could, making sure
if the worst ever happened to us, I'd feel exactly like this.

LEARNING TO BE ALONE

I'd convinced myself somewhat that Hunter was the source of love,
that Red was a mirror I could hold love up in front of, to check.

But just like that, I'm alone, have lost them both, differently.
My mother loves me a little harder;
my dad looks me long in the eye, telling me what a strong man I am.
It's as if they see an opening in time, an emptiness they can fill again.

I'm sad, but not too sad, finally, to speak, to smile back.
We've taken to watching movies as a family,
except Mom refuses to lie across us both, like I remember,
her head in Dad's lap, her feet and ankles heavy on mine.

She gives him an uncomfortable look,
as if they're not used to sharing the couch,
as if it's uncomfortable sitting side by side,
the three of us in a row.

But we pass a bowl of popcorn around,
until there are only the half-popped kernels, which only I like,
salty and hard to chew, but worth it. Satisfying.
Then like a kid, I suck on the seeds,
rolling them around like stones in my mouth,
all the while pretending to be scared for the good guys,
when all I'm really thinking about is
where I can spit these damn seeds
now that they're no longer salty.
One by one they hit the bottom of the bowl, clinking.
Then, all at once, I spit the rest out,
and they pour down my chin, like cement made of pebbles,
my spit having thickened among them.

I laugh, wanting so bad to be a kid.
But the look on my mother's horrified face pulls me out of it.
She has something to say, but she's holding back.

She's had something to say all along, something
she's been waiting my whole life to tell me.

I go to the kitchen and come back, all cleaned up,
the bowl washed and put away. But I can see it on her face
as she pretends to watch the movie. She's judging me.
"What?" I say, not caring if I ruin it.
"What?" I beg her, picking a fight.
I don't want to cry, but already I can't see, my vision blurring.
"Nothing," she says. "Calm down." Then she's sitting up,
sitting straight up, face forward, like she's watching the screen
and not me out of the corner of her eye. Dad says, "Watch the movie."

Now I'm really crying, wanting them both to see what they've done.
On the screen, the heroes have fallen in love for no good reason.
Yet there's a look in their eyes, like goodness will prevail.

I hold my breath as long as I can, until I can't breathe without
    it sounding
loud and dramatic. "Watch the movie," Dad says again, slowly.
But this time, he's saying it to Mom, too. And when I look up,
I realize I'm not the only one crying for no reason.

ANGEL

"Angel," I said to Grandma. And she said, "Okay."
Said, "That's easy to remember. You *are*."

And when her husband said it, he nodded.
He could nod at an angel, and I guess at me.

My teachers agreed, and Abercrombie—
though he said I'd stay a devil to him.

Vanilla thanked me for the note,
and hugged me so hard, it startled me.

But you, Hunter . . . why is it so hard to see what I want?
Or is treating me well the one thing you're bad at?

SHORTHAND

What I miss most, maybe,
is how he looked at me
like I had all the answers.

A bird landed on a power line,
and he asked what bird it was.
If it hurts to stand there,
a wire live in its claws.

He didn't *say* that. Vanilla didn't have to ask in words.
I knew from the way he lured my gaze
Vanilla wanted to be a part of the poem
I was writing in my head.

Or maybe he was fishing for words
he could quote back, reminding me always of us.

"Play later?" Vanilla asked,
which meant video games.
But what he really wanted was to lose fast
and lie down next to me,
the ritual of his promise complete.

"Sure," I said, "if Barb can come out."
His name for who I turn into
fighting no holds barred.

His smile was his answer, often.
The back of his hand tapping my thigh.
His temple at my shoulder.
His palm to the sunny sky, as if
checking for rain.

"I could lie like this forever," he said.
Then, "Okay, starting *now*."

Referencing our first date, and every reference since,
fastening the moment to others.
Those simple words I'd said once
sung back at me, like a mockingbird's taunt from its high wire.

"I don't mind when you tell me what you're thinking," I said,
flowing with him through our briefest script.
"Good. Because I like telling you."
I squeezed him hard,
my mind having become a record player.
The needle of my nap-numbed attention
focusing on the parade of memories
banked by that one familiar bit.

I miss how he asked to be spun,
how he asked without words to be reached for.
I miss the way he waffled
between menu items, then asked,
"What are you having?"
as if inviting me in on a deal.
I miss how I'd say, "Deal,"
skipping to the end, having predicted
his next move.

I miss predicting his moves.
Knowing them at all, I guess.
But more, I miss having a shortcut
into a person's affection.
A way to sever the ground right then,
and layer in another reach of vine.

"Your mom will be home soon," he said, as if starting a timer.
"I could lie like this forever," I said, quoting him.
"I'll see you tonight," he said, sitting up.
"I see you always," I said, refusing to.

WRITING TO HUNTER

I told him I deleted all his pictures,
and it's true that I deleted some.

The ones I kept are hidden
in the same place I used to hide others, back when.

It made him angry when I first told him,
and I ate his anger up

like it was the most delicious thing.
He forgave me, said he'd save them all, even the bad ones,

and that one day, when I regret it,
he'll gladly return us to me, no questions asked.

At the time, it felt like a cruel assumption,
and so I threw his anger up, again, to spite him.

But now that I'm forgetting what it was like to be loved,
I wish I had a few more. Already picturing a day

I'll send that email. Already bashful,
composing it in my head.

GRAND GESTURES

"Red," I say,
"how do I get him back?"
       "Can you?" she answers,
       then swallows it.

"Find the thing that ruined you
and ruin it back," she says.

       And I have my answer.

"What if I was just scared?"
I ask her
and Red knows
what I'm asking.

       "Were you?"

I nod.
"But I wasn't scared enough.
That wasn't why."

       "Why, then?"

I love Red.

Somehow
it's as if no one
has asked me before
       though of course
       they have.

"I didn't want to lose him,"
I say
even if it makes no sense,
especially now.

"I was scared of doing it,
but also of having done it.
It's like when he looked at me,
he saw innocence.

"He called me innocent
and so I thought
maybe it was the innocent part of me he loved."

        "You're hardly the baby Jesus,"
        she says.
"Bitch!"
And we laugh.

"I know what you mean, though."

"Yeah."

"And also?"
I say.
        "Yeah?"
        she says.

"What if I'm not good at it,
as good as what he imagines?"

        "Then you get good at it."

"We'd be doing it a lot, I guess."
        "Yeah, probably."

"That's maybe what I was afraid of, too."

        "Huh?"

"Having to lie,"
I say.

"To your parents you mean?
Your friends?"
"Both."

"That's sweet,
but it's not a reason."

"Yeah, it is."

"You'd only have to lie
if they make you."

"Yeah."

"It sounds like you
have your answer."

"Do I? I'm not sure."

"Is that really why
he broke up with you, though?"

"He says it's not."

"Then you should listen."

"But it's what broke us
even if it didn't
break us up."

"Still," Red says,
"Maybe you should ask him again.
Maybe his reasons have changed."

"And if he says no still?"

"Then you definitely
have your answer."

NOW OR NEVER

1

I had a dream that aliens came to Earth.
They cut patches of trees down, making room for their laboratories.
They were fascinated by the air. How it carried noise perfectly.
The first animal they met, they all wished they had mouths, had ears.
One alien transmitted a thought among them:
Oh, to be sung at! To sing to each other!
They took turns working their science on the animals,
divining a snippet of their nature into us.
What will it sound like for one of our kind
to sing like that? one alien thought,
and so they all did. Oh, their delight
as their first human song was born,
and the tones of our shared longings
were first felt upon their faces, and ours.
The sound waves pounded
like snow on a human tongue.
And they basked in each vibration
as if it were light. Hidden inside us,
they turned our faces toward the music,
then left.

2

When Vanilla came over, trying on friendship
like a favorite shirt that no longer fits,
I wanted to tell him about my dream,
but he said he didn't care about dreams anymore,
just our real future.
Then he tried to put his tongue in my mouth.

"What's wrong with you?" I said, pushing him away.
I didn't want to tell him about College Boy, or anyone else.

But Vanilla broke down anyway.
"I told you I was ready," he said,
though he clearly wasn't, flinching even as he said it.
All I could do was think of my dream
as I listened to the terrible music
of his indecipherable sadness.
Staring at the lump in his throat
as he warbled apologies,
trying to convince me all over again.

"Say something," Vanilla begged, and I told him I couldn't
without telling him my dream. The words felt insufficient in my throat,
explaining where my love had gone.
"It's there, still," he told me, not even a question, "somewhere,"
and he said not to worry because buried love can be dug out again.
But I cried. Making no sound. And Vanilla steadied himself.
"I'll prove it," he said, trying again to kiss me. Reaching for my crotch.
I clamped my mouth shut, not wanting to say something I'd regret.
Truth is, I didn't want a kiss. I didn't want him
to taste tears when he thought of me.
"Please," he pleaded. "I'm ready. I swear!"
"I hear you," I said, but I wouldn't let him touch me,
feeling suddenly like I hadn't slept in days.

MY PEOPLE

1

I've found them. They aren't mine,
but I am certainly theirs, made of the same stuff.
You can see it in our eyes, how we see the same true colors
and dance the same rhythms, really feeling the music.

I marvel at the happiness of our tribe.
Tribal less in its laws than in its loyalties.
Practicing for when it counts.
Our hearts are less meaty,
tendered by a shared nonviolence
as we put away each greed
for the sake of the group.
It's lovely, made of love.

2

Clown says to call him Angel, and I tease him
because at first I think it's his latest disguise.
Then he tells me he needs a break from us, and I know
it's "clown" that was the disguise all along.

I remember when he first took to wearing wigs to school.
Toupees, mainly, over his buzzed scalp—each a shock, even to me.
And though I thought I was in on it, I wasn't. I realize now.
Because they weren't a joke. Funny as it seemed. Even if he laughed
    along.

The first was a lavender-gray piece with showy curls in the front,
    pinned high.
The second was a wave of blond and strawberry, parted at the side.
Elvis bouffant. '90s spikes. Mohawks and bowl cuts in an array of
    colors.
Our teachers hate them, but only one puts up a fuss, threatening him

until he takes it off. She said, once, they were distracting,
and we all knew she meant they were distracting to her.
Since none of our classmates weighed in, aside from booing her.
Once, I caught Clown's eye as he took his hairstyle off.

He blushed as if I'd never seen his buzzed head before.
And I realized that it wasn't funny to Clown—to Angel, I mean.
He wanted the illusion to hold. And from that day since,
when Miss Bitch asks Angel to take off the day's toupee,

I refuse to look. And so, with at least one of us,
Angel gets his way.

3

I'm sorry.
I can't keep up, I say.
Which is a new fight.
Because I guess I've lost track
of everything but College Boy.
And I know Angel's right, because
the way I feel inside matches
what Angel sees. Only
the way he sees it,
I'm the bad guy.
Selfish in love.

PEP TALK

Abercrombie corners me at a party. He's good at it.
Slaps my ass and calls me "champ" like his coach might,
grips the muscles of my shoulders hard,
massaging them a little—at least I think
that's what he's doing. I'm not sure
if he's coming on to me. Maybe he's testing me.
I imagine Angel sent him to the bathroom
after me, to see what I'd do. Now that I'm not
only single, but infamously so.

"How you holding up, big guy?" he says.
And it doesn't seem like a test.
Suddenly I don't feel trustworthy.
Like I've been too cagey with Ab, too guarded.
A bad friend, even. "Do you mean
have I done it yet?"

Ab laughs, says,
"Damn," like he's scandalized.
"You need it bad, huh?"
Now he's rubbing my shoulders again,
working them hard with his thumbs.
"Hot guy like you," he says. "You'll get yours."
I watch him through the mirror.
His eyes are searching mine for something.
Vanilla used to gaze at me like that, pleading,
as if it were him asking for it
instead of me. He'd stare for as long as I'd let him.
I'd think, *What now?* Because
if it were me in control,
I'd reach straight for his fly.

"What?" Ab says, letting go.
I breathe out hard and he smiles.
"You're dangerous," he says, reminding me

of the night I met College Boy. But right now
the danger's all Abercrombie.

Maybe because with Vanilla
it was always me to lean like that
and always him to break our gaze.
With Ab, I lean right into it.
I turn to face him, stare so deep
I can no longer see him
or us, or how tipsy I am.
I kiss him, push him back
against the wall, until he practically is
my mouth. His lips opening with mine,
one smile. But then he's laughing
like a rocket pushing off
and I'm the ground
burned up under it.
"Damn," he's saying again.
"You *do* need it bad."

"Sorry," I say. "Don't tell Angel."
Then Ab's looking me hard in the eyes again.
"You mean Vanilla," he says,
but I don't.

LEARNING TO BE ALONE

Hunter called to read me a poem (go figure),
and it was so perfect in the moment
I knew I'd want to read it again.
Maybe even read it forever.
Like, on my deathbed, weeping.
It was about a horse with no saddle,
who wanted one so badly.
Like how Divine wanted her cha-cha heels.
Only that poor horse!
He was too lonely in his skin to gallop,
thinking himself naked when he was fully clothed.
And I was that horse once,
naked no matter what I was wearing.
I pictured the last words of the poem
coming out my mouth as my own final words,
the stink of a sterile room all around me.
Gasping for air as I went, satisfied.
I told Hunter as much, begged him
to send me that poem immediately,
right then while we were on the phone.
Already I wanted to read it again to myself
and know myself as that horse of Hunter's,
unbridled up until the end, and never grateful.
But Hunter said he wasn't sure if *he* liked it enough,
said he didn't want bad poems floating around.
I said, "I'm telling you I love this poem,"
and I'm not sure why I went there, but I did. I said,
"I'm telling you I love it, and I want it.
And I've done us both a favor for how long now,
never telling you I love you,
so you wouldn't have to deny me
having any chance ever with you.
But this poem is already mine, I love it so much.
Give. It. To. Me."
Then I said some other stuff,

nonsense to fill the silence, hoping he'd interrupt.
But he didn't.
He sent me the poem, though. And I thanked him.

I think I'm finally over that part of us.
But still it hurt so bad
that when I reread the poem, I hated it.
I hated that horse and hated myself.
Never happy with what I have.
Besides, it seemed gross,
a horse wanting a leather saddle,
strapped—or however saddles work—over the horse's back.
I hated the poem so much, I imagined
ripping a page from a book and balling it up.
But I was reading it on my phone and couldn't
bring myself to delete the email, telling myself
if I did, I'd be destroying crucial evidence.

SEX NEEDS

It's annoying buying lube
because even though it's legal,
people eye you from the pharmacy window.

If you hover too long in the aisle,
someone notices. And though they mercifully never ask
if you need help, they know you're there.
And, worse, they know why. Thinking any number of things.

Condoms are annoying to buy, too,
but at least there's a sense of accomplishment.
Look how safe I am, how respectable.
Lube's different. It just is.

Though both say, *See, I'm getting some.*
And both say, *So what?*
It's sex. Mind your business.
But both also say, *It's happening.*

Nail in the coffin.
First domino, tipping.
Whatever metaphor
makes you think of love
burned up
in the air between two people,
like what happens when something falls
too fast through the atmosphere.

My brother said I couldn't be sure
that College Boy knows what's up.
Meaning, it's up to me
to stock up.

Why is my hand still shaking?
Does buying it mean

I'm really going to do this?

Because I am, right?
I am.

AIRPLANE MODE

It isn't like turning everything off.
There's still music. A camera.
Only none of the noise.

Being with him is a holiday.
Nothing matters, not even us.

But I turn my signal back on, after,
and it's a wave,
too big to push against,

so I dive under.

Mom asks where I am.
Angel asks who I'm becoming.
Even Vanilla reappears,

wanting to meet me.
But why?

It's as if happiness has to be rationed
or else the universe corrects the balance.

I tell myself the only part that matters
is not drowning.

I FIGURED HUNTER OUT

In the poem, he wrote *you*,
and maybe he meant me
or maybe he meant the reader

or maybe he meant the ocean,
because of how it lapped at his legs
when we were alone at the beach.

Or maybe he meant the runner
who lapped him twice
as he refused to race,

the runner in another poem,
who stood in for College Boy, I think.
Or who stood in for Hunter,

who sat there
on his own shoulder,
judging himself.

Hunter might have written *you*
meaning the poem,
caught in time like a spring in a watch,

or the way he was trapped,
by freedom
instead of time.

Or maybe he meant Abercrombie,
if it's true Hunter kissed him.
True like nothing's true anymore.

Hunter knew
what he was doing
when he read it to me,

his car idling
so long it started to shake.
His hand on my knee

the only thing in that
hunk of junk
not shaking.

IMAGINING HIM, IMAGINING ME

Isolation takes its toll. The nights
my friends don't invite me to dinner,
the nights College Boy takes hours to text me back.
But worst is when I imagine Vanilla
idling outside my house,
his headlights out, my least favorite music blaring.

Some mornings I sneak out to drive
toward the nothing of dreams, minutes after waking.
All to savor the feeling of being intentionally lost.
Sometimes I curse myself
for craving that exact thing I've given up.
Other times, I remind myself what pain is for:
my body's way of telling me something
I need to remember.
I plug my ears and listen.

For longer spells, hours or afternoons,
whole days, even,
I seal myself in a kind of sadness.
I take a bath—not to be clean, but to be submerged.
I want to fight for breath, for life.
Bubbles tickling my nose as I close my eyes.
I pretend the silence I hear underwater
is a kind of noise, love's patient engine
revealing its voice to me like an animal
stepping bravely out of the woods.

I want everything I've touched to be gone
if he's gone, want everything good I've done
cataloged and put away, for my soul to be emptied
so that maybe it can be filled again.

You don't believe me? That love
has an engine? You think the body purrs

all on its own? It takes patience
to see light blink out of the dark,
silence to hear the leaf-crackle of arrival
as a deer lips the grass toward your dark porch.

Just my nose above the waterline,
I imagine he feels the same loneliness I do,
the break I gave him, gave us both,
a gift he might someday thank me for.
The kind of quiet that sharpens the senses.

I think of Vanilla settling into blame
until it's comfortable,
having to learn to see through tears,
like a kid underwater.

NO REGRETS

No regrets, I tell myself. Kissing new lips.
Feeling new arms. To him, I am young and overeager.
He sets the pace of our wandering, teasing me
each time I run ahead. To him, I am a racehorse
chomping at the bit, a runner bolting
before the gunshot. Bowler with his toe leather
slipping up an oiled alley. "Slow down," he says
when I dive toward his nipple, his shirt just over his head.
He wants to see my face, always. My hunger.
Sometimes friendly, sometimes cruel. But always astonishing
when he grips my hair or the scruff of my neck,
and pulls me up. I gasp,
then remember myself, my nerves still lit up at the surface,
sensitive to the air. "Baby," he says, "leave some for later!"
But the thing is, there's always more,
experience itself replenishing outward
so that after we've thrown ourselves
side by side, our red bodies pressed and still drumming,
I'll drink the very sweat from his neck until it tickles.
I'll grind against the stillness of his skin
until he begs me to stop, too spent and tired to stop me.
Then it's me, briefly, in control.

No regrets, I tell myself. Lying next to him, and becoming
a part of his rest, my own mind restless. Wanting
to start again always.
Because if I don't,
and my mind wanders, it wanders to you,
and what it would be like lying next to you again,
your familiar head
on my chest, like his is,
your ear against my heart like a cup
to a wall. Forgive me,
if you can, for running ahead,
unable to gauge the distance I've put between us.

I needed so badly
to know, and now that I do
I want nothing more than to show you
where I've been.
Because if this is what it's like without love,
feeling closer to someone than I've ever felt before,
imagine what it would have been like for us.

RENAISSANCE MAN

1

My handwriting has gotten smaller and smaller
until I can barely make it out.
On a field trip, Angel surprises me
by sitting next to me on the bus.
When he sees my writing,
he asks me if I'm a fan of da Vinci.
"The *Mona Lisa* guy," he says, as if he doesn't expect me to know.
"I guess," I say, not knowing much more than that.
Angel tells me da Vinci was gay, like it's a fact,
and that he used to write in his journal
upside down and backward
(or something like that)
so that the words were only legible
if read through a mirror.
"And mirrors were expensive," Angel adds,
which honestly wouldn't have occurred to me.

I close my journal and let him
lecture me about the Renaissance.
About polymath people, who were good at everything
in an age before our Age of Computers
made such knowledge unnecessary.
"Disposable," Angel says,
though that seems like the wrong word for it.
He goes on a rant
about the antagonisms of rival inventors,
"mad geniuses at odds," he says,
giving me a look like we're those geniuses.

"What's your secret?" Angel asks me,
pointing to my closed notebook. I tell him

I don't have one, but he doesn't buy it.
"Come on, you can trust me."

The thing is, I think he's right.
I used to think Angel was only nice to me
as a way to get to Hunter.
But he's nice even now,
when I have nothing he could want.

Angel is untangling a knot in his headphones,
which makes me think of Red.
His dark glitter nail polish shimmers
like water out from under a bridge.
"I know I can," I say, too late,
like a sigh to myself.
Angel smiles. "Good. Now spill."
Already he has the cord untangled.
Could put in his earbuds at any moment.

I tell Angel about Red, and how angry she got
when I missed the dance. And how she
didn't stop being my friend exactly, but stopped
being good at being my friend.
I watch as Angel's mind wanders
away from me, somewhere else.

"Do you think Hunter is a Renaissance man?" I ask,
thinking of all the things he's good at.
"Ugh," Angel says. "Enough about him.
I want to hear about *you*."
He sits lower in the seat, props his knees up
on the seat back in front of us. I do the same,
sinking down next to him.

"Okay," I say, thinking
Angel's not even digging, just talking.
Yet anything I might say about Hunter is dirt now.
I open my mouth and nothing comes out.
Angel smiles like he gets it.

"I don't like Hunter more than you, ya know. Not lately."
I almost don't want to ask, but it feels weirdly good
knowing I'm not the only person Hunter's hurt recently.
Because if Hunter's acting *so* out of character,
maybe it wasn't the real him who dumped me.

"He's changed. No biggie," Angel goes on, like it's all he'll say.
But when I leave it there, he picks it back up.
"I felt like we were close, but he's kind of disappeared."
"Yeah," I say, afraid to say more—because if I do,
I'm not sure I'll be able to stop. Angel gets real quiet.
"Enough about *him*," I say. And we both sink deeper.
Soon we're talking about when we were little,
and how we used to think of high schoolers as old,
and now we're practically adults but feel no different
than we did back then. He tells me how
he still eats sugar cereal and I confess there are some nights
I want nothing more than to watch bad cartoons
and eat peanut butter right out of the jar with my finger.

"Ew," Angel shrieks, shaking his head, then looking down
at the backs of his fingers. "I hate eating with my hands!"
"Really?" I say. And he nods. "Knife and fork, girl.
And spoon, obviously. And chopsticks." My mind is a blur
of cafeteria lunches and after-school snacks.
I rack my brain, trying to think of a time I've seen Angel
grip a burger or fold a slice of pizza like a taco in his palm.
A single image comes to mind of watching him
eat chicken nuggets, cutting each one in half
with the curved side of a plastic spork
before using it to dip each dainty bite
meticulously into sweet-and-sour sauce.

"Sorry," he says. "I know you don't like being called 'girl.'"
But I explain that was when I thought he was insulting me.
Angel gets quiet again, like I've said something wrong.
And if I have, I'd love to know what, so I could take it back.
"I know we're not talking about Hunter," he says,
"and I really don't mean to pry. So seriously shut me down
if I'm crossing a line . . ."

"Okay," I say, reluctant, expecting the worst.
Realizing that, right now, the worst would be
if Angel's digging after all, on Hunter's behalf.
That he's been sent here for a reason.

"Is there more to the story?" Angel asks.
"Because it doesn't add up."

It's the same question I've answered a million times.
But different, too, because it's Angel, who already knows
one side of the story. "He got tired of waiting,"
I say, because it's what I've been saying for a month now.
"I guess I should have just done it," I tell him,
searching Angel's eyes for an answer
to the question that's been eating me alive:
Would it have mattered?

Angel's watching my face, too.
I tell him how I threw myself at Hunter,
prepared to do what I was never prepared to do before.
"I didn't mean to make you cry," he says,
pulling out a handkerchief with a pink whale
embroidered in the corner, like he's been my friend all along,
but in a way all his own. Fairy godmother,
waiting for the right moment
to dazzle the air with his spirit fingers.
Even if I don't deserve it.
Even if I didn't make it easy on him.

"You know, I take it back," I tell him.
"If anyone's a Renaissance man, it's you."
I'm thinking of all the parties Angel's thrown,
the costumes and curtains and tote bags he's sewn,
his good grades and good looks and extreme confidence.
How he can be (and is) friends with just about anyone.
How he knows a little bit about everything,
from Leonardo da Vinci to how to fix a bike chain
without getting grease all over your hands.

"I mean, Hunter couldn't paint his nails as perfectly as you."
It's a joke, but I'm serious.
Angel smiles, looking again at his fingers. But the look on his face
goes hollow when he notices an imperfection
and then starts picking at it. When he finally stops,
he's quiet again, looking past me, out the window.
Far off to something out of his control.
"It's a compliment," I say. And Angel perks up.
But I can see it's for show.
"Spill," I say to him, so gently I wonder
if he even heard me. He says, "It's nothing, really."
But he seems almost afraid. And as I press the issue,
I watch as Angel recedes deeper and deeper
into himself. As if his body were a shell
and the true Angel were a snail curled up small inside it,
where I could never reach.

"Renaissance *person*," he says, eventually.
Quietly. Like he wants no one to hear
but wants to have said it.
And at first I don't understand.

"I'm not a *man*," he says. "I'm a *person*."
He doesn't sound angry. Or even chiding.
But he's serious. More serious than
I've ever heard him be.

"Renaissance person, then," I say, just as seriously.
"That's what you are."

2

On the bus back, I save the seat for Angel.
"Round two?" Angel asks. "Can you even?"
And I laugh, moving my backpack, making room.

"Did you see the naked mountain man?!"
Angel plays it up as if the painting had been scandalizing.

"You'd think Rick Tanner had never seen a penis,
the way he recoiled."

"Maybe he hadn't," I say, and we laugh.
"Or maybe he doesn't like foreskin," Angel says.
"Or maybe he prefers a shaved bush," I say.
Taking turns making the other laugh
until one of us takes it off the rails
and we're no longer making sense
but still laughing.

"You're twisted," Angel says.
"I can't believe I thought you were a prude."
"Thanks," I say.
Angel's knees go up against the seat back,
and mine do, too.
"Can I ask, then?
Why not do it
when you loved him?"

If it was anyone else asking,
I'd spiral into my shell.
But Angel deserves a real answer,
and besides, I know
Angel will believe me
if I say out loud
what I've known to be true
for long enough
but never dared say:
"I don't know."

We talk for most of the ride home
about times I thought I was ready,
only to find myself anxious,
no longer able to go through with it.
"It doesn't make sense," I say,
guessing it's what Angel's thinking.

"Maybe it does, though," Angel says.
"Not everyone has sex."

It takes me a second to realize
Angel is quoting me back to myself.
"It's true, though," Angel goes on.
"There's such a thing as asexuality."
I give Angel a look
like it's okay that I'm being teased
but it isn't that funny.

"Maybe you're asexual," Angel says, like it's simple.
"For real, though."

I think of biology class, straining to remember
the specifics of the word.
Cells dividing. Creatures multiplying
into clones of themselves. Angel
hands me a piece of gum,
and I take it thoughtlessly into my mouth,
reading the backward font
on the reverse of the backlit wrapper.
Feeling like da Vinci without his trusted mirror.

"There are plenty of people that don't feel attraction,"
Angel says. And I know if Angel's saying it, schooling me,
it's probably true.

"But I'm *attracted* to Hunter," I argue,
wanting so badly for Angel to be right.

"You think he's beautiful, because he is,"
Angel says. "People are attracted to beauty.
We want to be near it, surrounded by it
on all sides. But are you *sexually* attracted
to him?"

I think about a time on the phone
when Hunter had been jerking off,
telling me all the things we were
going to do to each other. And I asked him,
were we really going to do all of it?

And Hunter said yes, and my heart sank
because I wanted nothing more than
to do whatever he wanted, yet I had no interest
in doing any of those things, not ever.
I didn't see the appeal. I felt emptied
by the idea of acting out of obligation,
when the rest of our relationship
had been so true.
Pleasure wouldn't have been the word.
And if not, what would the word have been
if not torture? I simply didn't want it.
No matter how "good" it felt
to be hard. Or to come. It felt like disappearing
in a way, and I wanted if anything to be
more present with Hunter. Not less.

"Tell me, then," Angel says when I don't have an answer
about Hunter. "What celebrities do you think are hot?"
And I think about it.
"Don't just rattle off the obvious hotties, now.
Who do you *personally* get turned on by
thinking about them?"

My eyes widen. I don't know.
"I don't get aroused thinking of celebrities."
Angel raises an eyebrow, nodding
as if everything I say is being collected as evidence.
"Any of the paintings or sculptures turn you on?
What about Mountain Man? Or the marble
twinks with their bubble butts?"
I know Angel's kidding, but also not.
"I mean, I know there were plenty of sexy pieces . . ."
I say, defending myself. But Angel nods again.
"Just because you can recognize something as sexy
doesn't mean it turns you on. Did any of it turn you on?"
"We're on a field trip!" I blurt out.
"Were *you* turned on by any of it?"
"Yes!" Angel says, as if it were obvious.
"As was Rick Tanner, I bet."

I chuckle, but there's a wave building underneath it.
My mind is racing, searching for a time
I was aroused in the way people describe.
I think of being alone in my room,
or at the computer. Of touching myself
until I was gone. Of browsing sex
the way some people window-shop,
with no intention of buying anything.

I had heard the word *asexual* before,
and perhaps even in this context.
But it sounded like an excuse.
Like someone claiming to be allergic
when maybe they weren't officially.
Or saying they didn't like roller coasters
when actually they were afraid.

But if it's true what Angel is insisting,
that there is some portion of the population
that understands what it feels like
to love someone all the way in
and still not want to sleep with them.
If it's true that there are people,
healthy normal people like me,
who have accepted it,
then maybe I don't have to keep apologizing
to Hunter or myself or anyone else.

CLOWN

Vanilla and I sat together on a field trip.
And we got to talking for real.
At first I thought of him as Hunter
in sheep's clothing, a surrogate
for his ex. But Vanilla's different.
Which is I guess why I told him.

I was afraid he'd ask if I'd told Hunter.
And I'd have to admit that I maybe never will.
That I want Hunter to see me
a certain way, and that I worry
if he knew how I see myself
it would all have to change.
Including the dream I have.

Or that if I did, Hunter would call me a liar
for not having told him the whole truth.
Then I'd have to call him
a liar back, never having told me anything
true, maybe ever. Instead saying facts
from poems, which bend reality
like light through a prism.
Which might be beautiful
but isn't always sufficient.

Telling Vanilla, there was none of that.
Maybe because he'd never assumed
I was telling the truth. Though I always was.
Or maybe because he understood,
being on the queer side of queer himself.
Even though he hadn't known it,
funny as it sounds.

But still, after we got off the bus
back at school, and hugged and thanked each other,

waiting for our rides, when Vanilla saw my grandma's car
he pointed at it with his eyebrows. "Clown," he said,
"your chariot awaits." And I almost reminded him
not to call me that. But I didn't, afraid to break the spell.

TERRITORY

I knew

the way a spider does
trapped inside a glass cup

It knows

by the silence coming closer
by the stillness of the air

It doesn't breathe
as we breathe
and so our stillness

cannot approach a spider's

its body already a cage
equipped for solitude

The conversation ended
but my mind spun a web
circling the word

knowing it to be one center
of my vast life

where before
I had been boundless

and so centerless
too much to take
too bright to see

I kept thinking
this is not disorder
but order

This is not disease
but ease

If there is a word
for this stillness
then I'm not trapped

sitting alone somewhere
making a life of waiting

ACE OF HEARTS

Keywords: *ASEXUAL* and *ALONE*
Top Hit: *Love is possible, and with someone better suited for you.*
Keywords: *ASEXUAL* and *RELATIONSHIP*
Top Hit: *It helps to know what you're looking for.*
Keywords: *ASEXUAL* and *DATING SITES*
Top Hit: *The world is both big and small at once.*

There was fear mixed into joy.
Fear that I would never be the same,
could never go back to who I'd been
before I knew who I was.

Keywords: *ASEXUAL* and *MASTURBATION*
Top Hit: *The body is not broken, just wired differently.*
Keywords: *ASEXUAL* and *DAILY MASTURBATION*
Top Hit: *There is every kind of person, and you're normal.*
Keywords: *ASEXUAL* and *AROUSAL*
Top Hit: *There is such a thing as an empathetic turn-on.*

And then there was joy mixed into the joy.
Like dough rising, or soda foaming up.
I could unlock each memory and make new sense,
and in making sense of it, I could see myself in my life.

Keywords: *ASEXUALITY* and *REASONS*
Top Hit: *There aren't any, silly.*
And: *Be true to yourself, and keep an open mind.*
And: *If someone says so, does that make it true?*
And: *Why are you relieved? There's an answer in that.*

Keywords: *ASEXUAL* and *SEX*
Top Hit: *I don't understand what you're asking me.*
Keywords: *ASEXUAL* and *SEX ANYWAY*
Top Hit: *Why would you ask that?*
Keywords: *ASEXUAL* and *BREAKUP* and *GET HIM BACK*

Top Hit: *There are people you could love*
who could love you back better.
And: *To do so would be like losing a part of yourself.*
And: *To do so is your choice, but don't.*
And: *But you're only now meeting yourself, really.*
Give it time.

And then there was hope folded into the joy.
So when it rose, it doubled in volume.
I shut my laptop, conscious of my breathing.
Outside, it was starting to rain, and suddenly
I wanted to feel it on my skin.

THAT PLACE I'VE NEVER BEEN

1

I could be walking anywhere,
the sun on my neck, in pace with my shadow.
I could be in a boat, making wake,
the engine turning a blade, cutting the water.
Everything I've seen far behind me,
and everything heaven promises
up ahead still, just beyond the curve.
I could be a tourist in another country,
each worn stone in the road
worthy of an amulet.
I could be listening to the wind.
Could be relearning my own life through it
or through some stranger's life. How they transcend it.
I could be an adventure, or home finally. Anyplace.

And still I'd long to be
that place I've never been.
To lie alone with that landscape,
my valleys and hills matching yours.
To share a sky, the two of us,
and core, far down.

2

I work up the nerve to tell Vanilla
I'm heartbroken.
He tells me he can see it in my eyes.
Could see it last week on the bus.
And that he's sorry.

I tell him it's my own damned fault,
but he disagrees.

"It's like you said," he says,
and then he quotes me back to myself,
something about Hunter's beauty,
about Hunter being a planet
and us his moons.

And though I'm listening, I'm also not.

In English, there are sometimes two words, or three,
that all mean the same thing.
But this thing I mean to say,
somewhere between heaven and hell, where we are—
There is no word.
Earth, ground, planet.
All insufficient.

Vanilla and I are twin stars, burning.
But how do I say it right?

"We make our own gravity," I tell him.
But that's only half of it.

COMING OUT AGAIN

1

It's harder the second time,
because they think something's wrong.

It's like my parents had my whole life
to practice being surprised the first time.
Quick to say all the right things.
Mostly.

This time around, they look at me
like I'm something out of place,
which is how I felt
only days ago.
Before I found my place
without their help.

Angel asks how it went,
and I say my parents are like the tsunami
that hits after an earthquake.
A separate, linked tragedy.
Angel asks if I'm the earthquake.
"No," I say. "I'm the person
finally out of the wreckage
who they'll pull into the water."

2

I thought I was safe.
I did a practice run.

Angel played both my parents in turn,
never having met them.
And yet it was useful.

"I'm so confused. I thought you were gay,"
Angel said, their voice deep and fatherly.

"I am," I said, as if I was assuring my father.
"I'm gay-romantic. I'm attracted to guys emotionally.
But for sex, I prefer neither."

"Ummm," Angel said, sounding like any mother.
"Say it again. I don't understand."

"Not every person feels the impulse to have sex."
Angel nodded, forgetting to be my mom.
I knew her arms would be folded tight.

"That 'pull' people talk about.
I don't know the feeling."

"I know you got broken up with, honey,"
Angel said, though my mom would never bring it up.
"You'll feel it again. That pull. I promise."

"You're not hearing me," I told her, and Angel said, "Good!
Make them hear you!"

But I shook my head.
"Something's missing.
I need a prop or something."

3

"Celibacy," I told them, "is not having sex for a specific reason."
I didn't tell them why; I simply defined it.
"And abstinence is not having sex for a less specific reason."
My mother looked at me like she was tired of being schooled.
"You guys understand the distinction, right?"

"Yes, I believe we do," Dad said.
"Celibacy is like a nun not having sex, because of God's rules.
And abstinence is like your mom's sister

not having sex because she doesn't want to."
My mom smacked my dad's arm, hard.
"That's hardly appropriate," she said.

"Focus," I begged them. "This is important:
Those people sometimes feel sexual attraction
and yet stand by their choice not to. Agreed?"

"Sure," they said in unison.
"Well," I continued, "there are also people
who don't feel sexual attraction at all.
People who don't have sex for that reason."

"Okay," Mom said, like she was waiting for me to say more.
Like she had already figured it all out
(even though she didn't yet understand).
Still, she wanted it said. And so did I.

"People like that are asexual. That's what it's called.
And that's what I am."

They each looked at the other, neither ready to take the lead.
When no words came out, or smiles or sighs,
Mom told me she loved me, like it needed to be said.
Or maybe like it was no longer obvious.

KNEE-JERKS

Red, blinking
"Wow. Okay."

There are times when less is more.
This isn't one of them.

The Gang, laughing
"Boner shrinker." "You aren't gay after all?"
"I guess you weren't kidding before, ha."
"Hey, I could have told you
you weren't sexy." "Ha!"
"Good one, everybody."

My parents, disbelieving
"We love you, no matter what.
But, say it again, slower."

Hunter
"I don't know what I'm supposed to say.
Am I supposed to feel bad for you?"

No.
I sure don't. I'm happy, even.
Except.

There was the feeling
that it might matter. To you.

You know, the fact of it
separate from you.
Acknowledgment

that what went wrong with us
wasn't all me, like we said.
And maybe it's you, too,

right now
treating me
like this.

THREE STRIKES

I should have known better than to answer my phone.

I'm ready to be friends, finally. I'd even admit there's love, still.
But immediately, Vanilla takes charge. "I figured it out," he says.
Then tells me about a blankness he feels,

a silence where he's sure there should be music.
As if it wouldn't hurt anyone to hear such a thing.
"I don't know what I'm supposed to say," I tell him.

"You're not supposed to say anything. You're supposed to listen."
Strike one.

I listen, fuming at his redefinitions
of who he is now, and what we were all along.
And I'd easily accept the former, if not for the latter.

It hurts to hear him change our whole story at once,
as if every one of my advances had been an affront.
And then, as if redefining us back again, in a full circle,

Vanilla asks if I could love like that.
Making it my choice again, to love him
through his blankness for me.

"How could you ask that of a person," I say. "Of me, or anyone?"
And then it becomes a fight about theoretical people,
about theoretical love.

"I thought you'd be relieved," he says (strike two).

Then, "I thought you'd be grateful, knowing the problem wasn't you."
"In which case, you never really knew me," I say,
and when that doesn't hurt him, I tell him I have to go.

"You know, I guess I am grateful," I tell him.
"Grateful it's not my problem anymore."

I wish I had the calm to explain
what I'm actually grateful for now,
how hard it's been getting over him,
moving on without him, the whole time having nothing
to be seriously mad about.

Until now.

HOW DARE YOU BLAME ME

When we kissed, it was me   who leaned in first.
    And when we danced,   it was always my hand outheld
in invitation—yours   always the one more hesitant
    to hold or be held. Your head   more willing than your body
to be danced with. Loved.   How dare you question my role in it all.
    When affection was made, so often,   by me, alone in action.

It was a date because I asked,   no matter who paid.
    A dip because I held your weight.
How miraculous it must have seemed   to you, never having to
    put much effort in,   never the one to think ahead,
or heaven forbid consider   what the other might want or need
    and never dare ask for.

Surprise, here's a picnic basket!   Packed with your favorite foods.
    Surprise, here's a sparkler.   A lighter. A star.
The only gift necessary   the surprise on your face.
    You remember scenes;   I remember how they struck you.
    Double happiness   but different between us.
Yours the happiness of happenstance,   mine of will, of easy work.
    But the kind that makes things   fucking happen.

How dare you call me up now, like this   relief filling your throat
    and say, "Psych!   I was never into it."
How can you call someone you loved and say none of it was real, not ever.
    How should it make me feel
knowing the dude I pine for still   has taken it all back,
    including the one part I cling to,   saying never
all over again,   leaving me
    with nothing, not even   the consolation prize?

MANSION APARTMENT SHACK HOUSE

The night I told Ab I didn't have a gender
we pretended we were kids again.
We played games in the dark,
folding paper fortune-tellers
out of pages of dirty magazines.
"Cootie catcher," he called it,
poking me with its beak.

"Do you think I'm a slut?" he said
as it kissed my arm, first slowly up to my shoulder,
then everywhere, fast and hard.
He pinched my nipple, platonically, with it.
"It's okay," he said. "I kind of am."

"It's good work, if you can get it," I said to him,
not wanting to answer.

"Do you tink Mista White will duds me fo it?"
(The cootie catcher had caught his tongue.)

"He won't if he's really Mr. Right," I said,
wondering what it was about me
Abercrombie liked
but didn't like enough
to kiss me, not even once.
Not pretending, or "practicing," or being funny even.

"Why do you care what I *tink* anyway?" I asked him,
and suddenly we weren't playing anymore.
"I guess I don't," Ab said, nuzzling into my cheek
like Hunter used to.

I pushed him away, playing mad. Still I wondered,
how did we ever put faith in those games?
First you write your various futures on a piece of paper.

And then you whittle it down from there.
Which takes first believing
you know your full options
enough to write them down.

KING OF HEARTS

We haven't met face-to-face,
but already (knowing where to look)
I've met a boy who agrees
with my new definition of love.
And already he's said
if he could fly to me, he would.

Red keeps warning me
not to fall for anyone I haven't met.
And I promise her it's the idea of him
I love, if anything. Imagining a day
we might all know better
who we are. Or at least
what to call ourselves
in order to be found.

PLAYING DEFENSE

I have the paw of a cat on my neck, lately.
I'm afraid to move.

Hunter doesn't like that I talk about him
with Vanilla,
doesn't like that I shared
another half of my heart,
taking some of his half back
to keep a little for myself.

"Do you really believe in asexuality?"
he asks, as if I put Vanilla up to it.
"Of course," I say to him.
"It's a valid identity."

"But Vanilla?" he asks, rolling his eyes.
"It's another excuse,
another way to make me feel bad
for all the times—"

"It's not," I tell him. "For once,
it's not about you." (Burn.)
And then, "Think about it, Hunter.
It makes perfect sense."

"Can't he simply not be ready?
Just the way he always said?
Doesn't he want to fall in love?"

I shake my head, thinking,
That's what they used to say about gay people.

"I'm reminded of a quote
by Maya Angelou. The *poet*," I say,

"'When people show you who they are,
believe them.'"

ANGEL CALLS THEM "PARTIAL TRUTHS"

I don't tell my mom that College Boy's in college.
I know without broaching the subject
that she'd have all kinds of opinions,
my dad having been a few years older than her,
and always treating her like he knew better.
Up until he left.

College Boy asks me what it's like,
not having a dad around to hate me.
I'd always assumed if I still had a dad,
he'd love me better than my mom could,
busy as she is.

"Something good happens," I say,
"and I tell Mom the news, show her my report card
or the prize I won for a poem. Every time,
she beams with pride and hugs me,
before getting back to her business,
and I double her embrace in my head.
Thinking of my dad, as if he's there, too,
as proud or prouder. It isn't fair to her,
but it's not like I choose it. That feeling is just there,
even though he isn't."

College Boy wishes he didn't have a father.
He tells me what it's like never being good enough,
no matter how good your grades are,
no matter if you win a prize or not.
And I think of Vanilla's dad, how it's the opposite.
Affection pouring onto everyone in the room,
regardless of grades or accomplishments.
Everyone good enough to be loved. Even me.
And then I think of Angel's grandpa,
and how hard the old man tries
not to look ashamed.

Mostly staying hidden while guests are over,
afraid of embarrassing Angel with questions
or old-fashioned ideas.

College Boy takes the long way home,
weaving through the neighborhood adjacent to mine,
playing lost. And I tell him about all the fathers I know,
even the ones I don't quite.
Abercrombie's, with his super-young girlfriends.
Red's, who looks just like her,
which is to say
tall and ginger—hence the name.

"I hope I get to meet them," he says. "Your friends,
not their dads. Ha."
I struggle to picture it and can't.
Aside from being unsure
who my friends are anymore.

Maybe I don't want to picture it.
And if not, what does it mean, if anything?
What am I scared of
now that my piggy bank of a heart
is glued back together?

"I wish we were lost for real," I say.
"I wish I had no parents at all."
But I don't mean it.
My heart lurches upright inside me
for saying such a thing
and I recognize the feeling
as one I've felt often lately.
I feel it for the joy displaced.

Like when I tell him, "I love you, too,"
and then spend minutes
wondering if it ever could be true.

ALONE AT LUNCH

A kid, I'd scoop at anthills with a jar.
I'd watch the chaos through clear glass,
screwing the lid of their tomb closed.

Hours later, I'd marvel at what got built
while I was away: a filigree of tunnels
marbled with anxious motion.

Time itself seemed cruel. Not me.
I could barely stand to leave them.
But once I did,

the divided colony found its order.
One part instinct, another survival,
the ants had lifted themselves by lifting

whatever stood in their blind way.
Until after sorting through grains of grit
and burying their dead,

the ants in the jar
somehow made a home again,
there in the hell I'd sealed them in.

Eating alone in the courtyard yesterday—
or rather, sitting alone, feeding the ants—
I pretended I was a mountain in their landscape.

Then a benevolent god, dolling out crumbs.
I silently cheered the monsters on, amazed
by nature's resilience.

If I had faith, I could overcome this.
If I had a hive, a queen. If I had one soldier,
I might know what to do, or who to follow.

And if I looked up and saw the hand of God,
I might no longer blame Him
for what was made, already broken.

Instead, I closed my eyes and imagined
a world simplified by disaster.
One in which love was something I could carry—

either with me, always,
or out of my damned way.

SAINT VALENTINE

For every crush, every two-week breakup,
every love note riddled with insecurities,
I was their go-to guru, their reluctant sage.
"But all love is different," I said each time,
resisting friends' pleas for advice.
But they trusted me with their hearts
or actions, so long the one in love
and loved back—a rare thing at any age,
I suppose, but especially then.
"Just be honest," I'd say, my cure-all
for whatever stood in love's way, finding it had worked
for me. For Vanilla. For us. For our love.
"Tell her what you just told me," I'd say,
my hand to my heart.
Or, "Tell him you're sick of group dates. He'll listen."
But sometimes love doesn't work like that.
Sometimes they don't listen. And sometimes
people break up because they're not meant to be together.
A friend might have come up to me and said,
"I did that thing you said, and I got dumped,"
as if it were all my fault, as if
my advice was to blame. "I told you to be honest,"
I'd remind them, "and if you can't be, then it isn't love."
What I should have said was "Stop asking me!"
Or, "Aren't you better off?"
Having yet to go through a breakup.
Having yet to trade honesty for time to think.
If Vanilla and I were meant to stay together,
it would have been lies that saved us.
It was honesty after all that asked for more,
honesty that said, "No, I'm not ready,"
and honesty, too, that said, "I can't do this."
I think of those early days, venting to Vanilla.
I'd say "What do I know, anyway?"
And he'd call me Saint Valentine and kiss my hand.

"About love?" he'd tease. "You know everything!"
Then he'd use it to flirt with me, saying,
"Valentino, I have a problem. Help!
How do I tell my boyfriend I want more kisses?!"
He'd pout his lips and bat his eyes wildly.
"You know they beheaded Saint Valentine, right?"
But I'd kiss him anyway. I'd pick him up,
our lips still touching, and carry him to the couch
like in a romantic movie, and we'd kiss like that
for a long time. We'd kiss
until we were drunk on kisses.
Or at least I was. I'd reach those dizzy heights
where I can't think straight, forgetting myself,
the facts of my mouth dissolving until I'm bodiless and pure,
reaching through him toward myself, my spirit doubling
and redoubling, becoming unbound. All of me his
for the taking. Not thinking, not able to think, my body
would take it too far, reaching, groping, gripping.
Vanilla would always pull back
or push away or roll out from under.

That's what broke me, finally. I could take the waiting.
I could wait forever to be with him, to make him mine.
But not like that. Not when the rules of flight
made me an outlaw in my own skin—the rise itself forbidden.
It was as if he never wanted me to let go inside,
needed me to police us, not please us.
I said as much once, feeling honest. It was late—
late at night, and late for us—I said,
"Don't you trust me? What do you think I'm gonna do?"
And Vanilla said something about wanting to let go, too,
but not being able to, if he had to keep my wandering in check.
"That's fair," I said, but it didn't feel fair.
"Let's start over. I'll be good."
And I meant the kissing but I also meant more.
I wanted to take all of it back, if only I could,
so he wouldn't be always on edge.
Be strangers somehow, in the best way, and not
in the way we had become. "I should go," he said,

"It's late." And I heard it for what it was.
"Too late," I said. He was breaking us up
and didn't even know it.

HONEYSUCKLE

We're walking along a chain-link fence.
An ordinary day. Winter green brightening finally.
We have nowhere to go, nowhere we've said we're going;
we're simply walking.

"Remember that time we kissed?" Angel says.
At first Angel's kidding, then Angel's not.
I smile because, sure, I remember.
"I got hard," I say, because it's funny now.
"Sure did," Angel replies, lips pursed proudly.
I make a little kissy face, and let it melt slow
back into my smile. "Wonder what that's about."

"It smelled like sex in there; your body knew it," Angel says.
I nod, because it makes sense. Though I wonder
if it's true, and if so, if it's the only reason.

"Remember the look on Hunter's face?" Angel says,
still thinking of our kiss, I guess.
"Yeah," I say, not sure if I want to talk about it.
Remembering how I felt the next day, afraid
Hunter should have been more upset than he was.

"I think he'd given up on me by then," I say.
I think Angel had some other point,
but if so, it goes unsaid.
"I'm not convinced he's given up, still,"
Angel tells me, and it seems like a painful confession.
Insight I shouldn't have, for Angel's sake
or my own.

"Only one way to know."
We turn in place along the fence,
and I follow Angel, who's walking taller now,
stomping as if Hunter might hear us

coming for him.
But we pass Hunter's apartment right by.

"Where are we going? Tell me," I say,
refusing to take another step.
Angel says the park, pulling me by the hand
and leading me deep into the brambles.

"I feel bad," Angel adds. "It was a surprise."
I'm reminded of a time with Hunter,
just before we broke up.
How he dried his eyelids on his gloves,
and I couldn't be sure if he was crying.

Then there we are, Angel and me.
Standing there in the same place
Hunter had stood before.
Angel points to something I can't see
and calls it proof of Hunter's love.

SNEAKING OUT

I listen for Grandpa to go to the fridge,
and tiptoe down the stairs, not wanting to be seen.

"Where are you going dressed like that?"
Grandma asks, sneaking up on me.

When Grandpa hears, he cranes his head
around the doorway to gawk at me.

"I'm helping a friend," I tell them.
They're eyeing my old jeans, my boy shoes.

I'm not wearing anything I like, not even my face.
Knowing soon enough I'll be sweaty, dirty.

"You off to bury a body?" Grandpa asks me,
and I joke that, yes, I'm burying his.

Grandma scolds us both equally
while Grandpa gives me a wink.

"You look half-decent in that, Angel," he says.
I scowl until I'm out the door

and then I practice winking.

HONEYSUCKLE

I can't help but think of Hunter's poem.
The one about this very honeysuckle vine,
with new growth so tender it can be cut
with the press of his fingernail.
And I see Vanilla out here,
getting his hands dirty. For what?
Does he know if Hunter comes here still?
He isn't texting. He isn't texting me anyway.
He barely posts anything new.
He's gone, disappeared with College Boy.

The Gang is an orgy of Baby Abercrombies.
(Not an actual orgy, but) I feel awkward in it.
Without my poet prince
teaching me what's beautiful.
All I have is Vanilla's broken heart,
complete with Hunter's footprint, us both
sounding like Hunter in the weirdest ways.

I can't tell what parts of the vine are hard or soft,
but Vanilla seems to. "Spring green," he says,
giving deference to the words.
All of it seems new growth to me.
I can't tell where Hunter's work stopped
and where Vanilla's and mine begins.
So I stop, pretending to be tired.

Vanilla refuses to take a break
and I ask for a hand check, to make sure
his palms aren't bleeding. (They aren't.)
He bends the hardened vines,
threads each gap like a needle,
pulling the rough part through
until it's tight. Then he curses

when they all spring back
to where nature intended.

I'm used to having nails on,
makeup to freshen. I feel naked
and vulnerable, the bright sun on us.
When my pocket buzzes, it startles me.
I'm used to the sound coming from my purse,
not this sudden, jolting vibration.
It fires against my leg and I panic,
hoping it's Hunter, hoping it's not.

I don't want to drop Vanilla for him,
like a puppy dropping its bone, running to the door.
And I can't exactly tell him where I am. Who I'm with.
But I wouldn't want to miss my chance, either,
now that Hunter time is rare.

When I check, it's Ab asking,
Where'd you hide my cigarettes?

I reply, *You told me to hide them, remember?*
But all he writes back is, *Where?!*

We volley back and forth like this
long enough to punish him.
Then I tell him where they are.

Angel, yr the worst, he writes.
Then, *No. Best.*
But I hate you anyway.

And then,
I can't keep calling you co-host
if you never show up anymore.

When I look to Vanilla,
he's kicking at a pile of leaves,
shoots he's torn from the vines.

"Look what I did," he says,
like he's afraid he's hurt it.
I assure him, "It'll live."
And I truly am sure that it will.

"The flowers will be all he sees," I tell him,
thinking, *No one will be able to tell
we were even here.*

I DON'T WANT TO FEEL LIKE THIS FOREVER

1

Sometimes I catch myself
thinking of my father
and instead of blaming him
for leaving us, I thank him
for teaching me so young
not to trust a man.
And I think of Vanilla,
and how long I stayed.
And I know I have my father
to blame or thank
for the time I wasted
or spent so well.
Thanks, Dad,
for making me
hate not only the players,
but the field. The whole game.
If a man could truly love
and still leave, what good is he?
What good is love?
And if holding on
to love is a choice between
always looking for more
inside or always looking
for more outside,
then isn't that why
I dug in so deep?

2

Before I started dating Vanilla,
I had a kind-of girlfriend. Her name was Candace,
and I called her Candy. I brought jewelry to school

I'd paid for with Skee-Ball tickets.
For her birthday, she had a sleepover.
I wasn't invited, because I was a boy.
But her father invited me to breakfast.
I stood next to him in the kitchen
and helped him make pancakes
while the girls opened presents in the next room.
Her father showed me the "family trick,"
rolling each pancake up around the fork
to move them. And though he was probably kidding
when he called me family, it really meant something.
I remembered the trick for a long time,
without ever having practiced it.
Then on Mother's Day,
my mom's new boyfriend hijacked breakfast.
He chose the menu, the presentation, everything.
But he put me in charge of the stove.
When I showed him my trick, he said,
"What kind of pansy-ass shit is that?!
Flip it like a *man*." And minutes later
when he saw me doing it again,
he scolded me. "What is that?
You 'fraid of making a mess?"
Then he kicked me out of the kitchen,
even though breakfast in bed was all I had
for my mom that year. I cried in my room,
hurrying to finish her card.
And when it wasn't good enough,
I tore it up. "Give your mom a kiss,"
he said, but it seemed insufficient
next to how that jackass kissed her.

3

Vanilla's dad likes to tell the same stories over and over.
Vanilla would say that's all dads, but I think
his especially. We would all be at the table,
and he'd be rambling on. Vanilla would groan,
"Not this one again," and his mother

would put her ringed hand
gently on Vanilla's wrist. "He's heard it,"
Vanilla would say. And his dad would ask, "Have you?"
"I don't mind," I'd tell them both,
because honestly I didn't. And Vanilla
would say, "See, Dad?" His mother
would shush him. "You know there's no stopping him
once he's started." Vanilla would
shake her touch off, embarrassed for them both.
"That's why I'm stopping him
now, before he starts." But of course it was too late.
He'd tell whatever story, and no matter what it was,
or how many times I'd heard it,
I'd listen anew—enjoying how his father looked
me hard in the eyes, how he'd lean in close,
whispering too loudly
all the ways he loved his wife.
Even if it was a little creepy
how he looked at her, in front of us,
asking without asking. And her saying no.
It still felt good to be included like that,
to hear his version of everything,
which was always slow and descriptive.
He'd go on and on about his college days
or the year he spent in the Peace Corps,
doing things I'd never dare to do.
And by the end of each story, I felt like
I knew him. Knew myself better, somehow.
As if I had been there, with him,
for whatever adventure.
And it was nice knowing
exactly what it was like.
You know, having a father.

4

It's long enough after our breakup
that I've lost count. Mom's friends who I rarely see
still ask about Vanilla. And while

I used to say we broke up
X number of months ago,
now I say, "I don't know. He's not
really in my life anymore."
Then I change the subject,
embarrassed that I have let someone
I love disappear against my will.
I stopped feeling Red out,
fishing for information. It stopped
seeming fair. Now all I know
is what I hear, several times
removed. And even that, I
half ignore. Since it still hurts
that he's in the world,
becoming someone
I no longer know.

I ran into Vanilla's dad
on a grocery run. My mom
was making cupcakes
for her team at the office
and she thought we had
more eggs than we did.
I was that guy, running
down the aisle without
a cart, grabbing a dozen
too fast, so that two eggs
fell out, cracked open
on the floor with almost
no sound. I looked
around, no one had
seen—or so I thought.
Then someone
showed up with a mop,
a girl I recognized
from school. She
smiled, said it happens
all the time. And I
apologized, blushing,

happy not to be
scolded. I grabbed
a fresh dozen, their
fragility in the front
of my mind. I carried them
to the front of the store,
holding the carton
level and with
both hands. And
there in front of me
was Vanilla's dad,
buying batteries
and oatmeal. I
hoped like hell
he wouldn't see me,
but he did. And
I wondered, *Do you
hate me?* Imagining
him ferocious,
protective of his son.
But he smiled
right off, reached out
his hand. I shook it.
"How have you been,
son?" he asked.
I put the eggs down gently.
He must have
seen me shaking,
because he said,
"Whoa," and
grabbed me by
the shoulders.
"It's okay," he said,
but it wasn't. And
how could he stand
to hold me
like that, there
in the checkout line
while I heaved,

almost a stranger
to him now.
And for once
I wasn't thinking
of him only as a father,
or myself as someone
without a father.
I was thinking of
Vanilla only. Of
all the times
he'd said to me,
"You better not
let my dad hear us,"
as I started up
his shirt. "They'd
never find your body,"
he said. And here
we were, his dad
and me, looking
deep in each other's
eyes. Maybe thinking
the same thing.
How's Vanilla?
Wishing the other
might actually know.

FINDING AN OLD PHOTO

Nothing else in life
is like the flutter of impressions on the mind,
the dizzying calibration of memories recalled
following the surprise of a photo I once took—
the spun wheel ticks
against its imaginary stopper.
To see Vanilla in this photo is to see
our entire timeline at once.
He's wearing our anniversary shirt.
And from that I remember
hikes and homecomings, the thrill of peeling the shirt
high over his head. The feel of his dampening back
as he lay on my arm, falling asleep to a movie.

For once the universe simplifies
my spiderweb of understanding
down to this one strand.

Thank goodness I kept it.
This moment of memory now
part of the memory.
A flicker to see by.
My eyes begin again
to see the world that's actually there.

For the first time in months,
I feel proud of myself.
This time
for loving something,
even if it's no longer mine.

READING IS FUNDAMENTAL

1

The Gang has dared to throw a party
Angel wasn't told about.
I insist we were probably invited. But Angel knows better.

Just yesterday, Angel was over parties.
But that's before Angel heard about the invite,
how it said, *Boys Will Be Boys: Gay Men Only.*

Angel borrows my mother's most ridiculous sunglasses,
and we storm into Ab's party, spray glitter in our hair.

"Reading is FUN-DAMENTAL," Angel says,
pushing into the center of the living room,
looking like a '50s librarian,
pinkie already pointed.
Pushing Ab into a corner with it.

"You didn't think
I was going to find out
and read you for this?"

"Mama!" Ab says. "Be cool!"
Angel's lips go tight.
"You never come anymore. So I figured—"

"Words!" Angel shrieks. "Yet I don't
hear a damned thing." I take on Ab's fear a little,
feeling my body tense.
The guys are all laughing. But I can tell
Angel is actually angry.

"I'm sorry," Abercrombie says.
He looks at me to save him. But how?

Angel pulls the glasses down
to get a good look at what's
in front of them.

"You *are* sorry," Angel says.
"And let me tell you why."

Angel lays into him, defining what a "party" is,
until everyone in the room is laughing at themselves
for how lame they must look,
with their spiked slushy cups
and dye-blue mouths.

"That's what you get
when you leave Fun
off the invite list."

"Your name's Fun now?" Ab asks,
and Angel points the pinkie again.
Ab's hands go back up
in surrender.

2

I'm zooming in on Angel with my phone,
wanting to catch the end of the monologue,
when a guy comes up to me, someone I've never met.
He asks if I'm taking a video of Angel
laying into Ab like that. And I tell the guy, "Yeah,"
wondering if it's Angel he's interested in
or me.

"Can you send it to me, please?
I want to remember every word."

I text it to him, happy to be talked to, welcomed.

"What's your name?" he asks.
"So I can add you to my contacts."

His eyes are so cute
that I've forgotten who I am.

"Vanilla," I tell him.
"Really?"
"Yeah."

I know I could give him my actual name,
one Hunter didn't give me.
I could let him make up an epithet all his own.
But I'm looking at how happy Angel is to be star of the party.
And then I'm looking at the video playing in my hand,
thinking about how I'm something else entirely.

"It's a nickname," I tell the guy.
"You must like sweet stuff," he says.
"Yeah," I tell him. "Depending what you mean."

Still the guy seems interested.
I start filming him, and he waves.
Raises an eyebrow seductively
and offers me a sip of his slush.
I tell him, "No thanks," still filming,
and smiling so he won't walk away.
He sees me staring at the straw,
at his blue lips curling.
He isn't looking at my phone anymore,
though I'm watching him through it.

"I'm pretty vanilla," I say, like it's a warning.
I don't tell him I'm not vanilla in my ideas,
but in my actions. Not a prude
or a puritan. More a witness than a judge.
But neither, really.
Just me. Vanilla.
But from the way the guy is looking at me,
I don't think I need to.

"Sounds like a good time," he says.
"Holding hands?" he asks me,
and I say, "Sometimes."
"Cuddling?" he says.
"Cuddling's cool," I tell him,
wondering if he gets me
like it seems he might.

I stop the video.

FREEDOM, FINALLY

I was always someone to alphabetize my books.
I had a system—not for everything, but
for everything that mattered. Alpha
by last name. It made sense to me.
I could always find what I wanted.

And then the books, they multiplied.
I was often reading—more like always
pulling books from the shelf. It was a compulsion.
Like looking up the name of the movie
because no one at the table can remember
what it was called—even if no one cares,
even if that part of the conversation is over.

I allowed myself feelings, like reciprocal anger.
The numbness gone finally. The guilt. Even indifference,
shed like a skin I didn't know I had. Armor, I guess.
My organs were making real emotions again,
dumping chemicals into my blood without warning.
I'd finger my shelves, looking for the analog
of whatever it was I knew to be suddenly true.
Thinking, if only I reread the poem in my head
I'd feel at home in myself again.
Instead of sitting back in my chair
or cross-legged on the carpet, thinking
of ways to start a fight. Get him to say he's sorry.

It took too long, asking the poets
for their not-exactly-advice. By then
I had a short stack of thin volumes to put away,
and I hadn't read a word. That's when I decided
I could reinvent my systems.
I could do anything now. They were *my* books,
mine in the way my pain was, my pleasures.
No one else had a say. And it made sense

shelving the ancients together, and the Romantics.
Putting all the criminals together in one cell,
and the magicians beside them. Music makers
and sweet talkers. The sexys far from the scholars.
It needn't matter if anyone else recognized the layout,
as long as I knew it for myself. I could pluck
the exact string I needed, the exact moment
I needed to hear it.

That was the turning point. My waited-for
epiphany: My life had grown too big
to recognize it only through others'
oversimplifications. If I wanted to live
a full life, I would need to decide for myself
which signs to heed and which
to ignore. Because who cares if the formalists
were less rigid than the avant-garde?
All I need to know is where to look
when I need someone, not necessarily why.

WITHOUT LOVE

Of course I've pictured it. What it would be like, even now,
going to write among the honeysuckles
only to find Vanilla there,
lying in the sanctuary I built for us.
Ab says they go there. Now I can't stop thinking about it.

Sometimes I picture Vanilla alone, smiling, shy,
waiting to be found. Other times he's with Angel
or Red. Or some new, sexless boyfriend.
And though it hurts to imagine him lying there
with anyone but me, it also feels good,
picturing him happy again, how we were.

I close my eyes and lie back on my bed.
Imagine the sounds of life, let them fade into the fragrance
that surrounds me.

"Hi," he'd say. And it would be birdsong,
his familiar tone.
"Hi," I'd give him back, squinting up
from dappled shade.
"I got your poem," he might say, if I sent it finally.
"I'm glad," I'd tell him,
making room for him next to me.
His back would still fit perfectly
against my chest. His neck
would smell so much like vanilla
it could cut through the scent of all the flowers.

Here, there, or anywhere,
without love I'm a person only.
I fail myself, my attention spread too thin
across tender leaves. Or a lover's skin.
Sometimes, daydreaming,
it hurts too much to open my eyes
and still not see him.

OUR SPOT (NOW THEIRS)

I want to write Vanilla a poem while I'm here.
Tear it from my journal, leave it folded
among crinkled leaves.
But I'm afraid of what I would say to him now
if I let my heart grovel a minute more.

Instead, I write to Angel,
giving thanks
for taking care of Vanilla when I couldn't.
Stanza after stanza, I fail myself further,
unable to say what I mean.

It's as if there's a past and present.
And I can see the past is perfect, unable to be touched.
But I can see the present is permeable.
I could reach through it and take his hand.

I can't stand the feeling it's love
keeping me away. As if I'm not allowed to take
from happiness I didn't help create.

We changed each other's lives, I write.
Then I write it over and over.
But I don't tear it out of my journal.
It feels so good to put it in those words
that I know I'll want to read them again
for myself.

SAD PAPER TIME MACHINE

My name in his handwriting. That familiar scrawl.

Inside the envelope, a poem he "forgot to send."

He signed it, *Remember this?* And I wish I could.

Then four pressed honeysuckles flutter out. And I do.

Is it silly I tried to taste one? Or that I pictured him

pulling blooms from our secret spot in the brambles?

Silly or not, I texted him, feeling something like gratitude.

I'll always remember. Don't worry.

HOW I WANT TO BE REMEMBERED

There's a free concert happening in the park.
Angel and I have a picnic first in the spot that Hunter made.
Then we follow Hunter's favorite trail toward the band shell.
I confess that I'm hoping we run into him,
and Angel admits the hope that we don't.

I scan the ground, as Hunter would if he were here.
I wonder when I started to feel okay again,
when exactly the pain turned back into affection.
Not love—that's not what I mean. Instead, it's as if
I became able to care about Hunter separate from myself.

Angel asks why I sent Hunter my secret letter.
"You didn't write it for him, did you?"
Though I know I didn't, I might as well have.
In it, I explained myself. And that's what he needed most from me.
"No," I say to Angel. "But it felt good to send."

We're late, and as we exit the trail, I hear the opener
far off, thanking the crowd for their generous applause.
She says it's her last song, and then begins to play on a violin.
"What did he say? Did he write you back?" Angel asks,
but I'm listening to those first notes, lifted.

"I haven't heard from him since he got dumped," Angel says.
And the anger in Angel's voice pulls me back down again.
Not emotionally down. But my attention. Back to the ground.
The way I'm feeling, it's as if I'm lifted enough to lift my friends, too.
But I don't know what to say. Our pain was and is so different.

"Do you still love him?" I have to ask. I don't want to, but
it's the question swelling in me, like strings on the breeze.
"No," Angel's quick to say. "I don't think I ever did. Not really."
But after a few seconds of quiet, Angel adds, "Maybe I did.
But I definitely don't now. I think of him constantly, though."

"How do you know *you* loved him?" Angel asks moments later.
"I know how *I* know, or would. But I'm curious. Without sex,
how do you know it's that kind of love and not another?"
I spend the entire concert thinking about it. I don't hear a thing.
I want to say, "I just knew." But that's not an answer.

On the way out of the park, Angel avoids Hunter's trail.
Instead, we take the long way around, back to the main road.
I can't imagine not wanting to take the trail. Even in pain, I did.
That's how I know, I think. But I don't say anything.
Angel wants to walk me home, and I let them. Though we're quiet at first.

Passing the middle school, I of course think of Hunter again.
And of those early days, so confused by every feeling.
I think about how love grew up around us, with us. How badly
I wanted to be everything to him, in a way
I've never wanted with any other friend. Not even Angel, who I love.

I wonder if attraction makes it easier or harder to know a person.
Does Angel not remember clearly if their love for Hunter was real
because of hurt feelings now or false feelings then?
How do I explain how sure I am, when all the metaphors I've heard
assume sex, the way people do, the way the world seems to?

If I were Hunter, I'd invent my own metaphors. But I'm not him.
Instead, I let Angel go on about Abercrombie's new boyfriend,
how he seems so sure about this one. "He used the word 'exclusive,'
but I think Ab's just afraid of losing him. He's epically gorgeous."
We turn onto my street, and I'm only half listening.

The late sun has turned gold on the sidewalk. Our long shadows
stretch out ahead of us, racing me home. I wish I could know
what Hunter thinks of all this, of love separate from sex,
if it can be real or not. For me, at least. Not because I need his approval,
but because I'm curious if he'll remember me as loving him back, truly.

GRAND GESTURES

If I could take it all back, I wouldn't.
Some of it needed to happen.
Even if it could have come about differently.
What I would change, though, is the timing.
If only Vanilla realized his reasons earlier.
If only he knew himself better, early on, I think
I could have been a better boyfriend to him.
But could I have? Could I really?

I used to be surprised every time it happened:
Late at night, or immediately home from school,
I'd lose myself in the act.
Returning to my senses afterward, I'd remember myself,
remember Vanilla. It was like writing a poem,
how when it's powerful I know it is
by the startling realization
of who and what and where I actually am.
As if I had been transported, like in a dream—
only I was steering it, in control all along. Or was I?

Looking back at the past several months
is like reading a poem written in a haze like that.
There are parts I recognize and parts I don't.
As if someone else had done the writing,
held my hands to the keyboard.
It's embarrassing, how I begged, thinking
Vanilla was scared, only. How I let Angel weaken for me,
characteristic confidence pulled back
like satin sheets. Only to have me walk away,
leave Angel there, alone, twisting.
As if vulnerability were a gift.
Which it is, I guess. Yet I was so ungrateful.

When Abercrombie calls instead of texts,
I almost don't answer. Remembering

how I tried to kiss him, the look on his face—
proud and sheepish both, validated
but also as embarrassed as me,
as if my misunderstanding
revealed an uncertainty hidden at his core.
But remembering that look on his face
is also why I do answer. I owe Ab that much.

"Wanna host again?" Abercrombie asks.
And I tell him my mom's not going away,
that I can't throw a party and get away with it.
"Doesn't have to be at your place," he says.
"Angel's birthday's coming up,
and I know it would mean a lot
if you had a hand in planning something."

"Of course," I tell him. I don't even have to think.
"But are you sure Angel would want that?
I haven't been the greatest friend lately."
Ab says that's why he's asking.
"I've been kind of sucky, too," he says.
"But Angel's my best friend. I know him—them—
better than anyone. Trust me. It'll be good."

It gives me something to do, other than mope.
We meet at a diner and plan it out.
A surprise party in Angel's honor.
"I want them to know nothing's changed," he says.
"Both of them. Vanilla, too."
But everything's changed. How can Ab say that?
"It's my fault if Angel feels alienated," he adds.
"All The Gang's bullshit. Making it a boys' club.
We're going to be seniors. Time to grow up, I think."

I loop Red in, and the three of us get to work.
Red especially. I forgot all the experience she has,
Ms. Party Planning Committee herself.
Her energy is contagious. And before I know it,
I'm pulling an all-nighter in her living room,

attaching balloons to a twenty-foot pole.
We get dizzy, the three of us, inflating and talking,
until I forget that Vanilla and I have even broken up.

"Thanks for not punishing me," I say to Red,
hugging her goodbye in her driveway.
It's the closest I've come to admitting blame,
at least to her. But she doesn't take the bait.
"You and Vanilla, both," she says. "Just let it go."
And I don't know if she means the past or guilt,
the relationship or the breakup, or all of it.
"See you tomorrow," she says.
I let her leave it at that.

It feels good to go to sleep without touching myself.
Maybe that's a strange thing to say, but it's true.
I'm so used to jerking off before bed
that sometimes it feels like an addiction. A problem.
Something to ease me out of the day, into sleep, sure.
But also a way to dream before dreaming,
to deny myself reflection as I nod off.
But lying there, so tired, excited and scared for their reaction,
it's as if I'm all mind, pure spirit, bodiless.
A vehicle for their happiness, like I used to feel.
And it's pure bliss.

SURPRISE

It's Angel's birthday.
The two of us go to a movie, then ice cream.
I can't help thinking of Hunter and my first date,
because of the long walk through the mall parking lot,
and how comfortable I feel next to my friend.

Abercrombie texts, and Angel shows me the message, rolling their eyes.
Almost forgot what today was! Ab has written. *Happy Angel Day!*
Then he invites us both over.
"Do you mind?" Angel asks. And I do.
I don't want to share them with Ab or anyone.
But the way Angel asks, I'm happy to follow their lead.

When we get there, the TV is on. It smells like Ab's been baking.
"I'm making you a cake!" Ab says, welcoming us.
There's frosting on his finger, and he lets Angel lick it off.
"Vanilla!" Angel proclaims. "My favorite." Ab winks at me.

"I have a kind of present for you," Ab says.
But he's looking at us both, and I don't know why.
"It's in the garage." Angel looks at me, suspicious.
"Garage?!" As if the word is tainted with motor oil.
But there's a gleam in Angel's eyes, too.
Temptation. Mystery. "Must be real big."

Ab leads the way, and the three of us step down into the dark.
Immediately, I have a strange feeling. Like it's a trap.
Then the lights come on, and the music, and all around us
people are screaming, "Surprise!"
The Gang is there. Red, too. Her posse of lesbians.
And then I see Hunter smiling at me, uneasy but so sweet.

"What is going ON?" Angel says, slipping easily into the lead role.
There's a huge rainbow balloon arch. Laser lights. Party favors.
It reminds me of Hunter's story,

the fantasy version of our middle school dance. Only smaller,
scaled to fit in a garage instead of a gymnasium.
The surprise of it all fades, giving way to a parade of smiles,
welcoming embraces. But I'm still looking at the decorations.
I can see Hunter's hand in it all. His mind. Affection.
When it's our turn to hug, we do. I even kiss him on the cheek.
"Hi," he says. It's so simple. And yet, when he says it, I melt.
Feeling like friends again. Like there's a real future for us.

"Did you do this?" I ask him. But he shrugs off credit.
"It was a true group effort," he tells me. Then he gives me a tour
of the parts he's most proud of.

Red hugs me from behind. "We had fun," she says.
And that's when I realize it's also a party for me.
No one has explained it as such. Not in those words.
But looking around, I feel it. I'm part of the group again.
Not only because I'm Angel's friend. But because I belong.

"Can you believe them?" Angel says. I pull them into me so hard.
"I can, actually," I say. "It's the party you deserve."

Ab turns up the music and some of us start to dance.
Eventually Hunter pulls Angel and me aside.
He says he wants to apologize.
I want to tell him that I'm sorry, too. Sorry that I didn't know
I'd ever be okay again. And if I had, I wouldn't have taken it all so hard.
"I've been a horrible friend," he says. "I know that.
The both of you mean so much to me. I hope I haven't ruined everything."
Angel shakes their head, not wanting to hear it. But kindly, too,
insisting it's fine. But Hunter disagrees.
"You've given me so much. Given us both so much," he says,
as if speaking for us both. "I didn't always appreciate it at the time."

"Temporary insanity. Gotcha," Angel says.
"Having been slain by heartbreak myself recently,
I can excuse a bout of inward tunnel vision."
I take Angel's hand, wishing I could figure out
why I feel so proud of them. And of myself.

Hunter sees Angel's hand in mine.
"You two make a lot of sense as friends," he says.
But his grin falters and falls.
I reach for Hunter's hand, too, still holding tight to Angel's.
"You can make sense with us," I tell him.
"From what I remember, you're a pretty great guy."
I squeeze his hand, and he squeezes back.
I think of all the parties when we did just that.
A pulse, checking in. And by checking in,
saying so much without saying anything.

Then I send a pulse to Angel, who lets go.
"It's my party. I should mingle," Angel says,
kissing my cheek, then Hunter's.
"You owe me like a thousand texts."
Then Angel calls for The Gang
to get into formation. I turn to Hunter,
let go of his hand, but he doesn't.
I don't pull away, but I don't return his grip,
watch his eyes for the long second he lingers.

"Don't worry," he says, letting go.
"I'm through the worst of it."
He pats the small of my back, like he used to,
then nudges me toward the forming circle of our friends.
I take Ab's hand in my right. Red's in my left.
I watch Hunter slip in next to Angel, across from me.
Still thinking of Hunter's hand at my back,
how familiar it felt.

There's comfort in knowing some of what I loved
might last. Might return.
The rest can be forgiven or find a new form, or not.
Only time will tell what kind of friend Hunter will be.
But when I smile across the circle at him,
the one he returns feels familiar, too, and crucial.

"I love you all so much," Angel says,
and then we all raise our linked hands

and step forward, making the circle small,
cramming together.
"We love you, too," I say,
and the crush of us
fills with the sound
of kisses on air.

NEWBIE

Just when I thought
I knew myself

part of life leaps up
from the inside

letting me know
it's there.

It would be easy
to go on living
all the same.

But I don't.
I know better
than to think I could.

Instead, I change
in a good way.
Living some other

part of myself.
I see my friends
do this. And I

see strangers, too.
Each of us
is startled

and each of us
proceeds in kind.

I'm grateful to notice.
It makes me feel

like at any moment
I might open a door

and miraculously
you'll all be there.

WE WERE HERE

In ancient China, poems were like receipts of being:
If we were together and encountered a swan, say,
I might write you a poem about a swan,
whether or not I was a poet.

And if I came to your house and you weren't there,
I might nail a page to your door,
a poem I wrote about love or friendship, or both.
Or a poem I didn't write,
one about ships passing in the night.

And you would have to write a poem back to me
whether or not you were in a poetry mood,
one saying (without saying it),
"Yeah, I got your poem."
And you'd pay back every affection,
part honor and part obligation.
(Like we only did at our worst.)

But imagine the paper trail we'd have
if we lived or loved by those same rules,
having chronicled in words
each unrecorded action.
We would have filled books by now.
Long shelves, whole libraries,
with sweet-smelling pages
infused with your cologne.

Imagine, too, the crumpled arguments.
Poems jotted on the backs of flash cards
and history papers. Poems that lie
about what we want
for no reason.
Ones we would have written
without knowing yet

which words leave the heart sore
upon rereading.
Short poems, with no meaning
other than to prove we were still there,
still together.

There would be poems, too, harsher ones,
asking, "Where's your honor now?"
Poems in all caps blaring,
"I WROTE YOU A POEM; WHERE'S MINE?"
I'd want to burn those last poems
and undo everything.

And yet
if I could only read our first kiss again,
each early glance
unriddled in your trembling hand,
it would be worth those others.
If I could only read it all back to you now,
like a map back to Eden,
perhaps I could convince us both anew,
what honor could be, and friendship,
and poetry.

WHAT GRAVITY FEELS LIKE

1

Hunter prunes the tree above our honeysuckle.
Angel and I stand below, catching the slender branch
before it hits down.
It only takes one thick snip,
and the young thing falls
(like a feather made of wood and leaves),
hard into our arms—

                          and with it
falls full sun.

The three of us enter our shade,
a bright spot of light
now shining on the soil floor.
Angel reaches their hand into it,
holding out a palm of pinched flowers.
We each take one, and sip the nectar.

Angel lies down in my lap,
and Hunter insists on taking a picture.
I smile big for a moment
as Hunter considers his angle.
Then I let my face go slack,
relaxing my cheeks, my gaze,
as Hunter finally snaps it.

I want him to see me as I am. My eyes
probing the lens, fullhearted
but guarded also.

He passes his phone to Angel.
"Look at us," Angel says, and Hunter nods.
"Cute one, right? The light is perfect."

"Sorry I wasn't smiling," I tell him.
But they laugh, passing it to me.
Turns out I was.

2

"I want one of you two," Angel says,
sitting up, and swapping places with Hunter.
He puts his arm around me.
"You can do better than that," Angel says.
So I rest my temple on Hunter's shoulder.
He parts my hair with the tip of his nose.

I'm waiting for Hunter to draw me in,
to feel his breath pull at my scalp with the slightest sniff,
but he doesn't. Instead, he kisses the top of my head
and presses his cheek there. I can feel him
smiling at the camera. And so I do.

"Okay, now all of us!" Angel demands,
spinning in place and falling backward into us.
A frantic selfie is snapped as we crash together,
then another of us lifting Angel back up.
When we look, we see a blur of arms holding on,
the circle of light on our legs, the only part in focus.

3

I know we've come to a new place
when Hunter and I are alone and he asks me questions.
Less about us than about me,
and how I am now instead of then.

He seems fascinated by my perspective,
as if mine is the shadow truth of his.
Or maybe his is the shadow. It's hard to be sure
when his glances orbit instead of land.

"I had been picturing it as an emptiness," Hunter says.
"Something lacking, I guess. I thought you'd never feel full.
Now it sounds peaceful, and I'm envious in a way."
He calls the emptiness my *frontier*. Calls me brave.

"I'm embarrassed," Hunter says. "I knew you best,
and then didn't. Can you forgive me?"
And I tell him not to be embarrassed, that in fact
I'm glad to have had someone see me

the way he did. That he could only know me
as well as I knew myself. And that it isn't fair to either of us
to linger too long on what might have been.
"I guess I did know," Hunter says. "Deep down.

And so I'm sorry I wasn't the one . . ."
I let him trail off. Let the idea float there, inconclusive.
"I felt full with you," I tell him. Let it hang there
in the air between us, right next to what he's said.

"I guess we'll always worry about each other," Hunter says.
"That's what love is. Even the friend kind."
I tell him I wouldn't call it *worry*, so much as *hope*.
That we'll each always want the other to be happy.

Hunter nods, then shakes his head, takes the bait.
"More active than *hope*," he says.
"I can't leave your happiness to chance. Angel's, either."
We hug at the corner, where I'm so used to turning with him.

"I'll let you figure out the word for it," I say, knowing he will,
thinking maybe the word is *love*, like he said.
A gust of wind blows, filling the air with pine seeds.
They spin down so slow, it seems a challenge to catch each one.

ACKNOWLEDGMENTS

This book would not have been written without David Levithan. I mean that literally—and in more than a dozen ways—but perhaps most notably because I set out writing the initial draft of *Vanilla* with David in mind as the story's one true reader. I wrote my first book fifteen years ago (thanks to David) and published it (thanks to David), and then I spent all those years feeling like a "real" writer even though I wasn't actively publishing (in large part thanks to David's friendship and insight). There is no way to thank David fully in words for the role he's played in my life—as friend, editor, mentor, headrest. Instead, I figure the best thanks I can give is to write as fullheartedly as possible. Which I fully intend to do . . . and for as long as I can. Thank you for everything.

I would also like to thank the eighty-seven young asexual writers who blew my mind during the summer of 2015 when I was halfway through the first draft of *Vanilla*. The poems were pouring out of me, but the narrative itself felt stalled. At the same time, I was reading submissions for an expanded edition of *The Full Spectrum*, an anthology of queer nonfiction by young people (which I edited with David). A substantial number of the submissions were accounts of asexual experience, and as I poured through them, I quickly realized why Vanilla wasn't surrendering to the plot as I had envisioned it. Turns out I had written an asexual character without realizing it, strange as that sounds. Once I (and Vanilla) better understood that fact, the story I was telling naturally resolved itself—not as I had set out for it to, but in a way these characters needed. I'm not sure I would have figured Vanilla's truth out on my own, and I'm deeply grateful to those brave young writers who helped me to see Vanilla (and the larger world) more honestly.

Many thanks to my husband and champion, Nico Medina, who lovingly read the entire first draft aloud to me during my first revision and later let me read the entire final draft aloud to him a second time. Yours is the love I know best, and without it, I would know nothing.

Many of the poems in *Vanilla* are directly indebted to other poems. The poem "Diagrams" owes its form to the poet Brian Bilston; "Nocturnal" is in conversation with "Walking Around" by Pablo Neruda; and "Backing Away" found inspiration in the poem "Last Post" by Carol Ann Duffy.

I'd like to thank my family and friends for their unwavering support, especially those who had a hand in making this book what it is. I'm grateful to Heather Alexander, Jocelyn Casey-Whiteman, Enio Chiola, Eireann Corrigan, David Francis, Jeff Katz, Diane Schenker, Eliot Schrefer, and Jeffrey West for their early insights on the poems and manuscript. Special thanks to Audrey Ference, Andrew Harwell, Paul Legault, Ricardo Alberto Maldonado, Dan Poblocki, Michael Renehan, Anica Rissi, Brian Selznick, and David Serlin, for our conversations, which contributed lastingly to this book. Thank you to my agent, Kate McKean, and to friends Zack Clark, Nick Eliopulos, and Kendra Levin for cheering me on as only publishing insiders can. Thanks to everyone at Scholastic—throughout the company, truly—who had a hand in bringing this story to life. I'm deeply grateful to have *Vanilla* in the world.

Lastly, I want to thank Laura Heston. For getting to know these characters as well as they did. And for helping me dig.

ABOUT THE AUTHOR

Billy Merrell is the author of *Talking in the Dark,* a poetry memoir published when he was twenty-one, and is the Lambda Literary Award–winning co-editor (with David Levithan) of *The Full Spectrum: A New Generation of Writing About Gay, Lesbian, Bisexual, Transgender, Questioning, and Other Identities.* This is his first novel. He grew up in Florida, received an MFA from Columbia University, and now lives in Brooklyn, New York, with his husband. You can read more about him at billymerrell.com.